A Return to the Land of Kitty Tails

Linda Lehmann Masek

Kitty Tails II

ISBN: 9781098713584

All illustrations, including the cover art, is the work of the author, Linda Lehmann Masek.

Dedication

**To Bitty Tiger, Gray Lady, Snowball
and all of our Little Strays**

Love you Forever

Kitty Tails II

TABLE OF CONTENTS

In the beginning

My name is Maggie and I am a famous kitty author called Mag-ni-fi-cat. I came from a long line of distinguished kitties in the Land of Northern Ohio not far from Cleveland

This book is about my ancestors, Maggie, Tweaky, Libby, and other animal friends whose tales have been passed down to me over the years. It also includes a story about St. Francis, Patron Saint of all animals, and one about my mistress' travels to the far north to see the baby seals, and then there is…but you'll see them all.

I hope you enjoy reading them as much as I enjoyed living them in this Land of the Kitties.

Kitty Tails II

Mag-ni-fi-cat
and the Hula Hoop Mystery

Round and round, up and down. I watched as my mistress, Lina Kile, tried to balance a spinning hoop around her waist. The thing moved up, then down, then clunked to the ground!

"I dropped it again!" Lina turned to her best friend, Cheryl Martin, in disgust. "This year, 1958, is supposed to be the "Year of the Hula Hoop" and I can't keep it going for even five seconds!"
Cheryl was jiggling around with her own hoop but not having any better luck than Lina. I licked at a paw before finally moving to talk things over cat-to-cat, with my best friend, Spud. He was watching the girls with a puzzled expression on his little cat face.

"I just don't get it! What are they trying to do with those plastic things? Get them to balance in the air?"

I used my cat logic to explain. "It's the latest craze. Everyone is doing the hula even parents!

3

The idea is to see who can keep the hoop rotating the longest."

"To what purpose? A sprained back? The logic of it escapes me!" Spud turned in disgust to sit under our favorite poplar tree. I joined him there as we watched the two girls trying to balance their hoops.

I thought back to the conversation of the night before when Lina's mother had bought her daughter a hoop in the local Woolworth's Dime Store. Why it was called a dime store was a puzzlement since nothing in the place cost a dime. Yet the hoop hadn't been that expensive and the folk of ancient times, like a doctor named Hippocrates and the old-time Egyptians, used the hoops to teach dexterity, agility and physical fitness. Even the Native Americans in North America had used them for storytelling. Their hoops had been made of grasses; the hoops of 1958 were made of plastic, at least according to Lina's mother.

"I certainly am glad that cats have more sense!" Spud toppled onto his back in the warm June sunshine. "Imagine twirling that thing around your waist for hours each day! Why don't they try rolling them around instead?"

It really didn't make sense to me, either, and I am a very clever cat nicknamed Magnificat!

"They did roll them when the things were made in Europe centuries ago. And children back then

4

liked to jump in and out of the hoops as they were moving. Kids played in the street with them until cars were invented back at the turn of the last century. Even movie stars enjoyed hooping like Gene Autry on television." I thought for a moment about Gene and his horse Champion; Lina and Cheryl both enjoyed his television program along with the Roy Rogers and Dale Evans program every week. Personally, I thought there was too much bumping around on boney horses myself, but there was no accounting for the girls' taste.

"Hoops are still a mystery to me. Why would anyone like these things? They aren't good for a thing except getting heart attacks and dislocations!" Spud curled his feet under him and prepared to nap. I joined him, my eyes heavy with sleep and thought about the thousands of hoops that were sold every year since Lina, Moms and I had first seen one on the popular singer, Dinah Shore's Show. I yawned and looked across the yard to the two girls. They were still hooping it up next to the swimming pool and house where our rich neighbor, Alex Tolmer, a seller of the hula hoops lived.

I must have dozed but the scream from the pool woke me up. I sprang erect, my eyes searching the water. My mistress, Lina Kile had tumbled into the pool!

Cheryl was on the sideline shouting instructions about how to keep afloat. I knew this was useless

5

since Lina didn't like the water and had managed to flunk swimming class at our local YWCA the year before. I ran towards the pool, Spud at my heels and literally fell head-over-heels on the hula hoop Lina had left lying on the lawn.

A hoop! I batted it with my paw over in Cheryl's direction. Spud hesitated and then helped direct the hoop to Cheryl.

Pick it up, please. It was as though Cheryl could read my thoughts. She grasped the hoop, sprang to the side of the pool and extended the thing to Lina who was trying to keep afloat in the deep end of the pool.

"Here! Hang on!" Cheryl shoved the hoop at Lina. My mistress grasped the curved end and let her best friend drag her into shallow water.

"Whew! I thought I was a goner for a second there!"

Cheryl wiped the water from her face. "Me too! Thank heaven we had the hoop and it got left lying in the grass where I could get to it!"

I sat down as we all caught our breath. Then Spud and I studied the hoop thoughtfully.

"Well, this hoop certainly did some good today!" Spud chortled softly.

I thought quietly for a moment. "Yes, that hoop saved the day! And..." I paused as the significance of what had just happened struck me. "I guess I'll have to change my opinion about this hoopy thing not being good for much. It certainly saved my mistress." I watched Lina and Cheryl hugging each other before they each came and hugged Spud and me. Lina picked up her new hoop and held it lovingly in her hands.

I went over and gave the thing a sniff. I wondered in that moment if it were possible for cats to do the hula. I planned to try the very next day. And that…I thought to myself, was a fact!

Kitty Tails II

A Combat Cat comes Home

The first time Army Staff Sgt. Jesse Knott saw the cat was in the town of Hutal where he was stationed in Afghanistan. The gray tabby had joined a group of other stray cats and dogs that visited the outpost. This particular kitty seemed more friendly and far more trusting; unfortunately, this trust allowed the animal to be captured and abused by others at the outpost. When one day the cat arrived with a bleeding paw, Jesse Knott adopted him as mascot for the "Hawk Company". Koshka (cat in Russian) as he was called became a favorite with the troops who stopped often to play with him on their return from missions; the animal took the soldiers' minds off of their injuries which were often severe and permanent. Knott himself suffered nerve damage from an IED and a fracture of his clavicle. These injuries were in part responsible for Knott not being along on a foot patrol which was attacked by a suicide bomber. Two close friends perished and everyone was injured to some degree causing Knott to fall into a guilty depression for not being along.

Koshka seemed to know of his friend's anguish and distracted him with purring, patting and crawling around Knott in his moments of darkness. The massive distraction on the part of the cat worked causing the soldier to decide to take Koshka back home when he left Afghanistan.

The Stray Animal League in Kabul made the arrangements, Knott's parents paid the $3000. transportation fee and an interpreter volunteered to take the animal to Kabul and catch a flight to the United States. The plan worked after a two-week delay on the part of the interpreter; Koshka came home to be welcomed by all into his new home in Oregon. He stayed there throughout Knott's future deployment in Germany and settled into a happy life. Eventually he and Knott were reunited; the kitty received media attention and was named the ASPCA Cat of the Year for 2013.

Knott adopted other animals to help him through his medical difficulties including two other cats and a German shepherd besides a service dog; he also hopes to attend college. He credits Koshka with helping him to trust people once again. Many credit Knott with saving the cat but looking at the entire story, it can truly be said that these two friends saved each other.

Letter From Tweaky
With Love to My Dear Family

I know you miss me and I miss you, too. I'm up here with lots of other kitties and we play, sleep and lay in the sun every day. You only knew me for a year after I was rescued by some kind people who took me in off of the local streets and found me a forever home. You gave me a year that most kitties only dream of. I had a Christmas for the first time in my life with a tree where I crawled up and down with all kinds of ornaments that I could smack with my paws and watch as they swung back and forth. I had my own stocking hanging off the fireplace mantle and on Christmas morning it was full of goodies!

I had a cat tree that was great for hanging on by my paws and there were cute little toys everywhere. I had a piano that was fine for hopping around on to make kitty music for my family. I could eat at my smorgasbord of food where I had so many goodies to pick from, I just didn't know which to choose.

My three sisters and I played together or slept all day in the sun that filtered through my own private window, where I could watch everything that was going on!

I was never lonely and always happy. You changed my name from Tilde (ugh, I really didn't like it!) at the animal shelter to Tweaky, which was so cute! When it came time for me to leave you forever after I swelled up from the cancer that coursed through my body, you sat in the vet's office as my spirit left and I closed my eyes for the last time. You gave me a true funeral and I was buried with honor at the local pet cemetery, a place of love and caring with all the other very special animals. Your love and caring made me into a very special animal too and I will never forget you.

Please don't be sad. I'm so glad you came into the pet store that day and fell in love with me and I with you. Sometimes when I awake in kitty heaven I see a beautiful rainbow in the sky and I know we will meet again at the Rainbow Bridge where we will all be together again, this time forever.

Kitty Tails II

The Story of Alfie

My name is Alfie and I want to tell you my story. It is also the story of the wonderful people who adopted me and why I am now one of the happiest kitties in the world.

I don't remember much of why they did it, but I was thrown out of a moving car outside of an animal shelter for big cats...lions, tigers and others; it was called Noah's Lost Ark. The shelter is located in Berlin Center, Ohio and I discovered later that it is the home of abused and discarded animals just like me. This is their story, too and how things happened in their world, as in mine, that were shaped by events that led them to this very special animal sanctuary.

It was the first day after I had been thrown out and wandered into the parking lot; I was just lying there half-stunned from my fall from the car when a nice lady came and took me into what appeared to be a store. I learned later that it was the gift shop at Noah's Lost Ark which helped raise money for the sanctuary and care of all of the unwanted exotic animals who lived there. The founder of the sanctuary also offered tours for visitors and programs for school children who were interested in seeing the big cats and learning more about them.

I recovered over the next few days and began to prowl around. I was very timid and for good reason; besides my other injuries I was also blind. I was afraid if it were known, they wouldn't want me and I would be thrown out again on some local road. These people were completely different; they found out and didn't care! If anything, the people seemed to want me more than ever, a true miracle!

I know our beloved director Ellen Karnofel, whose work is inspiring to all humans and animals who meet her, has taken in lions, tigers, wolves, bears, many other animals besides me of course. She has been the driving force behind Noah's Lost Ark for a number of years. We all love her, naturally, as our staff welcomes each new arrival with joy.

Over the next weeks I listened and learned a lot about Noah's Lost Ark and the animals who live here. Their "before" stories show some of the worst sides of the human "animal"...the abuse and starvation of the big cats. Their "after" stories upon arriving at the animal sanctuary show some of the best of the human "animal" where fear and horror are replaced with love and trust, whether it takes a month, a year, or a century. Failure is not an option to the people here.

The before stories of many of the animals are heartbreaking, but also show how little humans actually know about the needs of my friends here. Many of the people think a little cute lion or tiger is just the cat to live in their home until the cat begins to grow. As panic sets in, humans begin searching for a solution; unfortunately, this frequently happens when they dump their oversized family pet wherever. Many of these animals suffer severe malnutrition which often brings on disease, blindness and hopeless aggressiveness. Some of these animals have been used as some sort of "photo op," earning money when they are sweet and tiny but being abandoned in many cases after living for years in cramped cages or even apartments. A big cat named Lionus had exactly this experience; it led to a stroke, tail biting and amputation before this poor soul arrived at Noah's Ark and received help.

Animals frequently live at other sanctuaries which, due to a lack of funds, can no longer support them. Some like Paris and Nicole end up at animal auctions where anything can happen to them. Sophie, part lion and tiger, came to Noah's Lost Ark from a humane society confiscation as did a bobcat named Bobbi. Many such animals are so malnourished that they develop a variety of serious diseases such as Dandy Lion, who may eventually require serious surgery for a fusion of his spinal cord and skull. Sometimes the big cats such as the Siberian Tiger named Tigger are a part of roadside zoos that go bankrupt for one reason or another. Other animals such as a black leopard named Abracadabra suffered malnutrition apparently to keep her smallish and useful to her owner on televisions shows. She became blind in one eye.

The mission of Noah's Lost Ark can best be summed up in words found on one of their lovely yearly calendars: "Noah's Lost Ark is committed to educating people everywhere of the escalating epidemic of neglected, abused and unwanted exotic animals. By model of bestowing safe havens for mistreated exotic animals, along with educational programs, Noah's Lost Ark is instilling compassion, respect and responsibility towards the preservation and conservation of all animals, ultimately safeguarding the natural environment for future generations."

It's important to remember that these lions, tigers and others are Kings of the Jungle as they live out their lives here in peace, happiness and security. I am a king too...King Alfie of the Gift Shop at Noah's Lost Ark and that is a fact!

A Pet Blessing in Honor of St. Francis

On or around the 4th day of the month of October, people all over the State of Ohio and elsewhere bring their beloved animal pets...cats, dogs, gerbils, birds, frogs and others...to a very unique event, a Pet Blessing in honor of a special saint, St. Francis of Assisi. A minister, priest or lay person invokes this blessing over each animal which will protect and provide safety and health throughout the coming year. Different religions honor this saint as parishioners bring their beloved companions to the yearly ceremony.

As the participants gather in a group, the priest or deacon moves among them and blesses each animal with holy water while reciting the words of the blessing over them:

"Blessed are you, Lord God, maker of all living creatures. You called forth fish in the sea, birds in the air and animals on the land. You inspired St. Francis to call all of them his brothers and sisters. We ask you to bless this pet. By the power of your love, enable it to live according to your plan. May we always praise you for all your beauty in creation. Blessed are you, Lord our God, in all your creatures! Amen."

A certificate of blessing with the beloved pet's name is then given to the pet parent at the end of the ceremony.

The question remains as to who exactly St. Francis of Assisi was that he should be remembered in this way. These animals that were given to man by God were made to be loved; His love is seen everywhere, but no more so than in the love of the animals He gives us to cherish and take care of. St. Francis, the patron saint of animals knew this; in his own words this intent is stated:"to inspire the hearts of people and stir them to spiritual joy."

The date of St. Francis' birth is not certain; he was born to a wealthy silk merchant and his wife in either 1181 or 1182 in Assisi, Italy. He lived the typical life of a wealthy young man of the time, a spendthrift who squandered money on whatever caught his fancy with rich companions. Francis became disenchanted with this life and joined the military in 1202. He was captured and began to reevaluate his existence. After having a life-changing vision he went back to Assisi before traveling to Rome; Francis followed the poor by begging alms at St. Peter's Basilica. At San Damiano Francis had a vision of Jesus who told him to "go and repair my house which, as you can see is falling into ruins." The young man took cloth from a store his father owned, sold it and offered the money to repair the Chapel of San Damiano. The money was rejected by the priest at the chapel and Francis was beaten by his father for taking the cloth. The incident ended with the boy renouncing his parent and his inheritance.

Francis wandered around Assisi, begging alms; he finally set about restoring the chapel at St. Damiano himself. He also aided lepers, the outcasts of society, living near Assisi.

In February, 1208, Francis was inspired by the Gospel story of the twelve disciples going up and "proclaiming that the Kingdom of God is at hand." Francis preached to the everyday folk of the area which attracted eleven followers; the group wandered around Umbria preaching the Gospel of the Lord. This group of friars was endorsed by Pope Innocent III which was the official beginning of the Order of St. Francis (Franciscan Order).

St. Francis was determined to spread the Gospel throughout the world. He tried to travel to Jerusalem and Morocco but was thwarted by a shipwreck and illness. In 1219 he journeyed to Egypt during the Fifth Crusade; he had hoped to convert the Sultan to Christianity. A legend relates that St Francis challenged the Sultan's "priests" to a trial by fire in which the saint was not burned, but this has not been confirmed.

St. Francis returned to Italy where he involved himself with his newly formed Franciscan Order. In 1221 he continued traveling throughout Italy where he had a vision on the mountain of Verna shortly before the end of his life.

St. Francis had a special attachment to nature; he has been called the saint of the environment. He loved all animals and in his Canticle of the Creatures he talked of "Brother Sun, Sister Moon, and the Stars, Brother Wind and the Air, Sister Water, Brother Fire and Sister Earth". In 1228 Pope Gregory canonized St. Francis two years after his death. St. Bonaventure spoke of Francis saying that "He who called nothing on earth his own, owned everything in God and God in everything."

The following is a prayer to St. Francis for all living things:

"St. Francis, you loved all living things calling them your brothers and sisters. You have been named the patron of the environment. Help me follow your example of respecting and caring for all of creation, for our air, water, forest and all creatures, particularly for our pets. Watch over our world St. Francis, and help me to care for all living things. Amen."

St. Francis has always held a special attachment to the people of Northfield, Ohio, where a Pet Blessing the week of October 4th is extremely well-attended as beloved pets are blessed by  the statue of St. Francis close by the parish shrine to the Blessed Virgin.

This miracle shrine was created by the first pastor, Father Bernard P. DeCrane after he was appointed in 1956. The statue and shrine have been the site of many noteworthy stories including the story of Chatterbox.

Chatterbox was a reddish-brown squirrel who lived by the shrine and the eventual site of the statue of St. Francis; she ran in front of my car which passed over her. The baby squirrel was stunned and I took her home for the weekend where she recovered. I returned Chatterbox to her home by the shrine and watched while she ran happily off.

I returned many times over the years and left bread, birdseed plus other squirrely goodies. I never saw Chatterbox again although other squirrels...black, all-red and crème...inhabited the area. Chatterbox's tree decayed and collapsed over the years, which went by very quickly.

St. Francis of Assisi with the Animals

Many years later I stopped on one of my visits. I had seen a change in jobs, the death of my grandmother and the successful publication of my first Mag-ni-fi-Cat book. My eyes searched the trees before leaving the goodie bag I had brought.

When I turned to leave a surprise awaited me at the top of the shrine.

Three squirrels sat there, the exact image of the Chatterbox from so long ago, beautiful reddish brown animals perhaps six months old. They stared at me, completely unafraid and I could see the recognition in their eyes. They knew me!

It has been said by Carole Wilbourn, noted animal therapist, psychologist and others that animals communicate with each other, such as cats, dogs or horses. Was it possible that Chatterbox had told her squirrel family what had occurred and they had passed the story down over the years? Chatterbox had recovered, flourished and was saying "Thank you" for the gift of life that she had received so many years ago in the garden of St. Francis of Assisi, the patron saint of animals. I would honestly like to think so.

The following prayer is a beautiful tribute to a very special saint:
"Lord, make me an instrument of your peace,
Where there is hatred, let me sow love.
Where there is injury, pardon,
Where there is doubt, faith,
Where there is despair, hope,
Where there is darkness, light,
and where there is sadness, joy.
O Divine Master, grant that I may
not so much seek to be consoled, as to console;

To be understood, as to understand,
To be loved, as to love;
For it is in giving that we receive;-
It is in pardoning that we are pardoned;
And it is in dying that we are born to
eternal life."

Maggie's Miracle

She is a beautiful black Burmese kitty with flecks of gold in her dark eyes. My mother and I adored her and she loved us as only an animal can love, entirely and without conditions.

Maggie was a survivor having come to us from a cat slaughter and euthanization of animals place in

Akron, Ohio; cats were killed there for no other reason than that they existed. A daughter of a friend was a cat rescuer of these poor souls and brought my Maggie to us, only five weeks old, adorable and wanting only to love. She adapted well to our house and her three other "kitty" sisters and has brought us nothing but joy for the last sixteen years.

My mother was the one who found it on a dark day in March...the lump on my Maggie's back. I heard about it on the way to a very special church named St. Barnabas in Northfield, Ohio, where miracles had occurred in the past. The first miracle was in 1956 when the pastor, Father Bernard De Crane, had been trying to raise money by having the first festival to help finance the new church. The sky let loose a veritable flood of water on the first festival day; in despair Father and his helpers knelt and prayed at the newly created Shrine to the Blessed Virgin Mary. The rain stopped and the skies cleared as the storm moved out of the area. The festival made money and the new church was built.

There were other later miracles of course, when the robe on a statue of the Virgin changed color from a pristine white to a dark blue, bringing visitors from near and far. A statue of Saint Padre Pio was observed by a prayer group crying tears from dark eyes, real tears miraculously coming from the surface.

I stood in front of this statue at the Shrine to the Blessed Virgin and prayed for a miracle to help my Maggie, that somehow the lump would be benign and that she would be fine. I returned home and found my kitty. Maggie lay on her heated blanket and raised a dark head when she saw me. I felt slowly along her back and then felt carefully all over her. Maggie was looking at me oddly as though she wondered what was wrong. I could find no lump anywhere, it was gone!

A rational explanation of course was that it was a piece of litter or food that had gotten stuck in Maggie's dark hair but as I stood in front of the beautiful lady at the Shrine the following day,

I knew in my heart that it was not this. The lump which could have been malignant had vanished as though it never existed. I knew to whom my

Maggie owed her cure, the Blessed Virgin who adorned the Shrine at St. Barnabas Catholic Church. She had heard my prayer, answered me and cured my kitty on a glorious day in March.

Tommy and Rosie: a Kitty Love Story

The dark closed around my head as the image of the horrible boys faded, boys that had mistreated me before throwing me out of a moving car into a parking lot. I heard them laugh as they drove away; I dragged myself painfully along in the lot. My stiff, aching body relaxed. I had gotten away and was safe! As the dark closed around me I closed my eyes to wait for daybreak and new hope.

The sun was high in the sky when the kind lady found me. She got out of her car and took me into the building that bordered the parking lot. I saw a sign, The Purr-fect Place.

She carried me in, put me down and offered food; I was ravished but afraid and I scooted back behind a large piece of high-backed furniture to peek out at the ladies as they came and went. I was so afraid and the image of the nasty boys was all I could see. I stayed behind the chest to venture out at night and hide during the day.

It was a nice shop with clothes, antiques, glassware and many other things. People came and went at the antique store; they brought things for the volunteers to sell to get money for helping homeless animals. There was even a lady who wrote books and left some to sell, many about kitties just like me!

I ventured happily out at night and ate the food the kind ladies put out. I continued to hide during the day, although they spoke softly to me and even brought other kitties into the shop to tell me everything was now fine.

I hid for over a year but one lady with a musical voice, Melody, caught my attention. I eventually came out and everyone seemed so glad! They even brought a little friend to keep me company. Her name was Rosie. As I stared into her face, she purred and looked into my eyes. I stared back. I knew in that moment I would love her forever.

Forever was a number of years; my Rosie and I lived together happily in the shop. Other homeless cats came and went home with people who smiled, patted me and loved us all. I was truly happy for the first time in my life.

It had to end of course. I sickened as my body gave out to the ravages of age. My Rosie stayed by me and promised to never love another. As I closed my eyes for the last time an image of a rainbow-colored bridge appeared in the sky. I knew at that moment we would meet again someday and be happy forever.

A Wanderer Comes Home

The days and nights slipped past in a warm haze one right after another. I lived on the streets begging handouts from the locals in Florida, I and my stray buddies who had no homes either and merely existed day after day.

Some humans were kind to us of course; one of these held out a hand to me, picked me up and gave me a home! His name I found out later was

Perry Martin; he was a retired K9 officer and he loved me on sight. I loved him back as I had a place where I belonged for the first time in my life. I was taken to the vet for shots (ugh! Not so good!) and to have a little microchip imbedded so I would never get lost again. Perry nicknamed me Thomas Jr. or T2 and the next two years were the happiest in my life.

A bad storm, Hurricane Jeanne, struck our home. There was no power and it was so very hot. I saw an open window, tried to cool off and scooted through. Something awful happened then and I got lost again! My home seemed to have vanished and I couldn't find my best friend, Perry, no matter how hard I tried.

The days and nights passed in an endless stream of unhappiness as I wandered in despair on the unfriendly streets. Perry had gone; he thought I had been hit by a car so he moved away to Ohio and elsewhere before returning to Florida.

The years crawled past and one night as I sat hungry on a local street in Fort Pierce, Florida, a strange man approached. He picked me up and took me to a local shelter for homeless, unwanted animals. I sat in a cage and watched other poor ones like myself; we all looked hopeful every time someone entered the place. It was never me who got chosen.

The shelter people were kind and treated my fleas at a local vet. They also discovered my microchip from fourteen years earlier.

One day as I sat hopefully watching the door, a familiar figure from days of yore walked through the door. It was Perry Martin! The shelter people had identified him from the microchip. He still loved me ever so much and had come to take me home!

We got together on some computer thing called Facebook, my Dad and I. Lots of people celebrated because we looked so happy and we were 'cause I had found my way home. I had waited fourteen years and it was worth every second; I had found the one who really loved me and that made all the difference!

Kitty Love

My name is Magda Blaine and I am a kitty who was named after a character in my human mother's favorite television series "The Name of the Game" first shown back in the late 1960's. Perhaps we both had a similar history since the Magda of television fame, played by a beautiful Academy award winning actress named Anne Baxter, was rather a downtrodden member of society who had no home. This is how I started my relationship with my "mother", Linda, when I was abandoned in her neighborhood and taken in by a kindly owner of one of the many "kitty houses" in the area for animals such as me. I never knew why my previous owner threw me away but I ended up being loved in a temporary home. I would travel to Linda's place to eat the yummy food she put out, food her own three kitties didn't want. The neighborhood strays gorged themselves on Medley, Fancy Feast and Appetizers as we happily ate around the front porch where the food was served in white plastic dishes.

For this reason I stayed close and when I had a litter of five white kittens, I had them around Linda's back porch. I used to peek through the windows at her kitties and one day she spotted me! Linda was thrilled about my kitty family and put out even more food when my babies stopped nursing.

One day a gigantic machine came into the yard; it made horrendous noises and shot the long grass high into the air. I had been nursing my family but was so afraid that I took my babies and escaped, back to my original home in the Kitty House. Here the kindly owner found homes for my five babies as they grew into beautiful white kittens.

I felt sad as I said "Goodbye" one by one, but knew they were going to a better place with good people who loved them. Then it was my turn! I was taken to the local pet store by volunteers from an animal shelter called Forever Friends. As I relaxed in the store's cool air conditioning, my eyes widened in recognition; Linda came into the store to buy snacks for her three kitties. She stared in delight as she saw me resting in my private cage and came right over to rub my neck and coo softly to me. She told me how beautiful I looked and what a grand job the volunteers from the shelter had done. It must have been true because the next day my new owners appeared. They looked at me and fell in love. I entered into the second of my nine lives in a new home with a new name, Kitty Love.

Little Rupert,
a Very Special Baby Deer

It has been said that "There is no dishonor in failing, there is only dishonor in failing to try." This can certainly be seen in the story of Little Rupert, a baby deer, and the staff at the Tiggywinkles Wildlife Hospital in Buckinghamshire, England. Les Stocker who founded the hospital reported that Little Rupert's mother had been killed by a car; her baby was delivered in a miracle operation and placed in an incubator. The deer was a mere six inches in size and was barely over a pound in weight. The little animal was tube fed and for the first five days showed signs of recovering from the loss of his mother and the caesarean section performed to save his life.

Unfortunately, Little Rupert was almost three weeks premature and had problems breathing and digesting food since his organs were not completely developed. His eyes had opened and the staff was optimistic that the baby deer could recover, but there were too many odds against him. Wildlife recovery is unpredictable at best since wild animals are different from tame ones and respond in different ways than those raised by people.

So how did the story of Little Rupert end? He may have passed away at the Tiggywinkles Animal Hospital, but still lives on the Internet where his story and his pictures have been seen all over the world for the last ten years. The little deer remains in the hearts and souls of those who read his story. The people who tried to help him that day so long ago live on too through their efforts to make this world a better place, particularly for a special baby deer named Little Rupert. They may have lost the battle to save his life, but they didn't lose the war since they did their best. Little Rupert knows this and is smiling down on them from the Rainbow Bridge where they will see him again someday in the distant future.

The Story of Jasmine

An animal who has had her share of a hard life is a Greyhound dog named Jasmine who was found by the Warwickshire, England police cowering in a shed. The dog was an orphan left to starve and die after having been abused by the people she trusted. The police, feeling sorry for the wretched animal, took her to Geoff Grewcock's animal sanctuary (Nuneaton Warwickshire Wildlife Sanctuary) hoping that the staff there could restore the dog's health and confidence in people so that an adoption would be possible.

The staff embarked on this difficult job and achieved their goals when Jasmine was restored to health. During this time the dog's true nature was revealed; she felt a closeness to all other animals, perhaps because of her own difficult life and liked nothing better than to play the role of adoptive mother with new arrivals at the sanctuary. It didn't matter if the orphans were wild animals like foxes, owls or badgers or tame ones like dogs, cats or rabbits. Jasmine welcomed them all with a lick and broke the ice to regaining their trust, affection and confidence in the future.

The type of animal orphan seemed to be unimportant to Jasmine, the Greyhound; what was important was that the new waif needed help and that love plus affection could bring a cure to a homeless little soul, very much like Jasmine herself once was.

Jasmine's greatest triumph of love was with a tiny roe deer named Bramble; the baby deer responded to her foster mother's love as the two became inseparable and forever friends. When one day Bramble had recovered and could be returned to her forest home, Jasmine knew that her job in this case was over and moved on to the latest victim of abandonment or abuse arriving at the sanctuary. The loveable Greyhound has successfully found her place in the world of God's creatures and for this all involved are grateful many times over.

The Story of Molly

Molly is a true inspiration as her story demonstrates, when she was abandoned by people and managed to survive the major hurricane, Katrina. The pony was eventually rescued and taken to a farm; while there she almost lost her leg after being attacked by a vicious dog. Molly was determined to survive her injury; a subsequent infection caused her leg to eventually be amputated below the knee. She learned how to walk using a prosthesis to which she adjusted and learned to even like. Many times Molly extended her amputated limb so the prosthesis could be attached. Her vets have described this loving little pony as tough and determined to survive in spite of the odds which all seemed to be against her.

Molly has a new job since losing her leg; she and her current owner travel to hospitals and nursing homes. The little pony is a constant source of inspiration to people who have serious problems,

a pony who is still in love with life in spite of her horrific injury. Her story tells others that hope really does spring eternal and no matter how bad things are, there really is a new tomorrow.

<u>Noah the Dove</u>

Often people believe animals don't have feelings-
of love, sorrow, pain or joy. This is obviously not
true as shown in the story of Noah the dove. Noah,
a pigeon living at the Wild Rose Rescue Ranch in
East Texas, has become a foster mother and
nurturer to the many orphan animals

brought to this shelter. In the case of five bunnies
who were attacked by a dog only three survived
but these were disoriented and confused; they
were not given a good chance for survival.

59

Noah saw them and was lying by the open cage door when one of the bunnies discovered him, crawled over and went peacefully to sleep under his wing. Eventually all of the baby rabbits adopted Noah who has cared for them and other rescues, cooing and telling these tiny orphans that all is well and they do not have to be afraid anymore. Things are going to be just fine!

A Good Samaritan from San Antonio

A good Samaritan named Michael who worked in a second-floor office building in San Antonio, Texas, had a chance to play the Good Samaritan and save a family of ducks at the same time. The ducks unwisely set up their home nest on a planter awning outside of the office where Michael worked; the little female duck faithfully sat on her nest until the eggs hatched one afternoon. Mother Duck had to get her babies to the nearest water which was not going to be easy since they weren't old enough to fly. She edged over to the end of the perch and flew down to ground level. Here she enthusiastically quacked to her babies to follow.

The first duckling toddled to the edge, leaped off and then crashed on the pavement below the office building. Michael looked on in horror as Baby Number 2 toddled over to the edge. The Good Samaritan sprang into action, rushed out of the building to catch the obedient duckling before it died from a fatal fall. In true baseball style he caught Duckling 2 and set it carefully down by Mother Duck and her first offspring, still groggy from the plunge over the building edge.

Michael's coworkers were hanging out of the office windows, cheering the young man on as he successfully caught eight more babies; then realized he could hardly leave the mother and children on a busy San Antonio street. His coworkers provided a box to collect the ducklings; Michael then walked slowly toward the nearby San Antonio River, with Mother Duck trailing in his wake keeping her brood in sight.

It had become a complicated maneuver at this point with other office staff, bystanders and police involved. Mother Duck trailed Michael and her babies to the river. Here she took charge, quacked loudly and leaped into the water. Ever obedient, her brood followed as their mother circled in the river collecting all ten of her children who had survived the great adventure.

The young man reported that she quacked loudly almost as though saying "Thank you" before she and her ten children paddled up the river. Their great adventure ended on a very happy note due to a Good Samaritan named Michael.

Lil Bub,
a Very Special Needs Kitty

My name is Lil Bub and I am a most unusual kitty, not just because I am so dwarf-like tiny with small limbs or that my little tongue hangs out all of the time or that I am a girl with no teeth. I was born the runt of a litter of feral felines in Indiana and met my human, Mike, when he was in a very bad way bankrupt, depressed and desperate. We looked at each other and fell in love; he saved my life and I saved his as we became inseparable over the next five years.

Mike took some pictures of me when he hit rock bottom, mainly to give himself something to do. People saw my little cat face on Facebook and Instagram and liked me as my image was flashed coast to coast. Several shows like "Good Morning America" and "Today" contacted Mike and my career, which he handled, took off; I starred in two movies and many fundraisers and I became as popular as Morris the Cat and a sourpuss cat called Grumpy. The height of my fame came at CatCon in Los Angeles where a red carpet was rolled out to greet Mike and me! The event was filled with all things cat: tee shirts, toys and advice about everything from fostering kittens to owning a grown feline. The main topic was how disabled kitties like myself can make fantastic pets and have just as much love to give as normal kitties.

When Mike and I are finished at a fundraiser we return to our hometown in Bloomington, Indiana. Usually both of us are pretty tired emotionally since so many people meet and greet us and tell us how inspired they have been by us and by what we have accomplished. When we are not making appearances, Mike works in his recording studio which has become a successful business. And me? I do what all kitties do when not eating or sleeping or inspiring my human- I supervise, naturally!

Love you

Euclid Beach Park and the Feral Cat Project

For a seventy-year period, Euclid Beach Park (1895-1969) was perhaps the most famous amusement park in the United States. People flocked to the shores of Lake Erie in the Collinwood District east of Cleveland to sample the rides, the famous frozen custard and the beach. The park had serious financial difficulties until taken over by the Humphrey family of Cleveland who upgraded the beach, rides and general atmosphere making it a "family-friendly" place where people could bring their children and relax. Although there was a dance hall, alcohol was prohibited; there was also a dress code. Many of the rides were updated including a carousel with fifty-eight horses, seven roller coasters including the Flying Turns, Racing Coaster and the popular Thriller. These upgrades by the Humphreys kept Euclid Beach financially sound until the 1960's.

Several of the popular rides were sold to Cedar Point and elsewhere but unfortunately the finan-

cial problem was not corrected. The park finally shut down in 1969; the famous carrousel was eventually moved to the Western Reserve Historical Society where it remains today, giving people a sample of the joys of the park as they circle around on the beautifully designed horses. A few structures from the Euclid Beach Park remain including the well-known arched gate and the pier. A trailer park sits where thousands of people rode rides every year while on the site is a feral cat colony whose unwanted residents are cared for by several dedicated volunteers. Over one-hundred of these strays are fed and protected, being neutered or spayed at the Cleveland Animal Protective League while homes are sought. A nonprofit organization The North Collinwood Feral Cat Project, works to help these orphaned animals, truly the only survivors when the former Euclid Beach Park closed for all time and the season permanently ended.

A Squirrel Named Karl-Friedrich

I am not a cat or a dog but a baby squirrel named Karl-Friedrich, who has had a thrilling time finding her way to an animal rescue center. My mother and I were separated on a busy street in Germany. I thought I saw a man who reminded me of her so very much and I chased after him but he didn't understand and called the police when he couldn't outrun me! By the time they arrived I was so tired I just had to lay down to rest and then I went to sleep.

The police thought it was amusing that a grown man would be afraid of a tiny animal such as myself since I was just trying to find another mother with a home and didn't want the fellow to feel threatened by my efforts. They took me into police custody and then to the animal rescue center where I joined two other squirrels who had also lost their mothers. What happened then was simply amazing! An American broadcast news station picked up on my story and sent it over the whole world. Now I am famous! I can stay at the rescue center since they have been so very kind and I will have a home with loving people forever.

Trevor a Celebrity Duck

My name is Trevor and I am a duck, a very special duck, who was named after a New Zealand politician called Trevor Mallard. Why did this happen? Because one day after swimming for miles I found myself on a far distant Pacific island named Niue. This island doesn't have a lot of animals and the people here took one look at me and loved me on sight. I get fed all kinds of goodies, corn and rice and get ever so much attention from everyone on the island. In addition I also get attention from people all over the world since my story has been written and produced by the BBC (British Broadcasting Company).

I am very happy here but the natives feel that I should have company- another duck to keep me from becoming too lonely. They even talked about building a wooden mallard! I think it is a good idea; a very pretty little female ducky that I can talk to all of the time. Other people are concerned because I have only a puddle to swim around in since the island of Niue gets little rain.

73

People are bringing me water for my puddle so that it doesn't go dry! They are afraid that I will leave but I never would go. They love me and I love them and that is the most important thing of all, even for ducks!

The Adventures of Cheeto
A Story Poem

Once there was a baby elk who lived with his mother on the banks of the Snake River in the state of Oregon.

The baby elk was a very curious little elk and was always getting into trouble because of it.

75

"No," said Mother Elk as her baby put his head into some flowers and got stung by a bee,

"No," said Mother Elk as her baby stuck his nose into a robin's nest and got pecked by the robin.

And "No! No!" said Mother Elk as the little elk peered into the Snake River where he lived to see his image.

"You will fall into the river and get carried away," said Mother Elk. "I will never see you again!"

So the little elk tried to do what his mother said.

He stayed away from the flowers so he didn't get stung by the bees.

And he stayed away from the robin's nest so he didn't get pecked on the head.

But he liked to go down by the river and watch the water. And he liked to look into the water to see what was there.

So he did!

When the little elk peered down, he could see the fish swimming.

And when he peeked down he could see a frog hopping.

And when he looked down he could see a duck paddling away in the water.

And it seemed as though they were having so much fun!

One day when the baby elk came to the river, it was very still and quiet.

The water was smooth as glass.

The little elk didn't see the fish swimming, or the frog hopping, or the duck paddling. He peered farther and farther over the water.

And then, he saw another baby elk!

It had large brown eyes and brown hair and looked just like him!

It moved when the baby elk moved and it stomped when the baby elk stomped!

The little elk was so excited, he peered farther and farther over the river!

He forgot what his mother told him about never going in the water.

He wanted so much to be friends with the other little elk in the river!

Suddenly the little elk slipped...

And slid into the water with a gigantic splash. He coughed and sputtered and tried to swim to shore!

He thrashed around in the water and cried for help!
But he was too far out in the river!
And nobody heard him!

The river that had seemed so smooth and
harmless from shore washed the little elk away
from the bank.
It washed him down the river toward the rapids!
The little elk tried to swim back, but the current
was too strong!
He tried to call for help, but his mouth filled with
water!

All the time the river took him away from his
mother and the place where he lived.

The water pulled the little elk faster and faster!
And farther and farther!
And deeper and deeper away from the shore!

The baby elk looked up and saw a moose drinking from the shore before the river swung him around.

He saw a herd of deer hiding among the trees as the water dragged him on.

Then he spied an old red weather-beaten farmhouse as he was pulled by.

Then he saw the river rapids up ahead! He cried out again for help!

But it was no use!

The river pulled him over and under,

And around and thru,

And then under again

Before the baby elk washed up on the far shore.

The little elk got up slowly and looked around.

He was a long, long way from his mother and where he lived.

He didn't know how to get back!

The baby elk didn't know this part of the river at all! He didn't know which way to go.

Baby Elk was lost and...it was getting dark!

So, since he was hungry, the little elk ate some of the grass growing by the river bank.

He thought about his mother and how much he missed her,

And he began wandering along the shore, trying to find a way home!

As the baby elk wandered around a bend in the river, he saw two men sitting in a boat, out on the water.

The little elk stopped to watch as the men caught a fish and pulled it into the boat.

Then one man rowed the boat toward the bank and pulled it out of the water for the night.

Baby Elk was very curious about the two fishermen. He watched as they went over to their tent and made supper.

He watched as they made a campfire and cooked their fish and drank their coffee.

And he came closer and closer to the men. Until…

One glanced up and saw him!

"Look," said the fisherman, whose name was Frank. "Look, there. A little reindeer!"

"That's not a reindeer," his friend, Dave replied. "That's an elk! They live north of here on the river. There's a whole herd of them!"

The baby elk watched the men as they watched him.

He was a little afraid of them, but he was nosy, too. Then one of the men held out his hand with something in it!

It was a yellow, flowery-looking thing. The baby elk came over to eat.

"He's a friendly little guy," Dave commented. "And he likes these Chee-tos. That would be a great name for him. Chee-to!"

"See if he's still here in the morning," Frank mumbled. "I'm tired. Let's go to sleep."

Baby Elk watched the two men carefully put out their campfire.

Then he watched them lie down and go to sleep.

The little elk wandered over into some bushes and lay down. He was tired from his long day.

He wondered how he would ever find his way home.

The next morning, Baby Elk saw Dave and Frank pack their tent into a small pickup truck.

They had breakfast over the campfire.

And then they offered the little elk some more food, just like the night before. They offered him more Chee-tos to eat.

Little elk gobbled them down since he was very hungry!

Then Frank went over and backed the pickup truck around some bushes.

Dave loaded the tent and the fishing pole into the back.

Baby Elk watched slowly because he was very nosy! He wasn't afraid of the men anymore either.

When Dave offered him more Chee-tos, the little elk followed the man up a ramp and into the back of the truck!

Baby Elk watched as Frank got in the truck and started the motor.

He was a little nervous as the truck started to move.

But Dave kept giving Baby Elk his Chee-tos. And Baby Elk forgot all about being afraid!

Baby Elk peered out and spied the farmhouse as the truck went by.

Then he saw the herd of deer pass by.

Finally he watched the moose go past.

Frank drove very slowly for a long, long time.

Baby Elk peered out anxiously.

Suddenly he became very excited! He saw some trees that looked very familiar!

And he saw some red flowers with bees in them!

And he saw a robin's nest with the robin sitting on it.

And then he saw his mother looking nervously at the truck.

Frank stopped the truck and Dave lowered the ramp.

Baby Elk jumped out and ran past the flowers and past the robin's nest and back into the meadow on the bank of the Snake River where he lived.

He ran back to his mother, who was so glad to see him!

And Baby Elk knew that he was home!

Dear Reader,

There really is a Chee-to and he really does live on the banks on the Snake River. After his mother died, Chee-to had to fend for himself alone in the wild. He survived his first very cold winter and became friends with the many fishermen who frequented the area. In summer, he met the boat captains who ran the sightseeing tours up and down the river. Chee-to would come out into the water and actually greet the boats, welcoming families into his part of the world. It was in this way that the author encountered him while she was on vacation.

Chee-to is friendly and trusting and all of the boat people fell in love with him. And yes, he really does like to eat Chee-tos!

The End!

The Story of the Little Strays

The huge round eyes stared into my own, horrified and afraid and ready to flee. Kitty eyes. I looked out of the glass in my front door; they looked as though the poor animals were starving. This was confirmed moments later when the group scurried over to the bird bread I had left on the grass moments earlier and began tearing it into small-sized chunks.

"Wait!" I thought rapidly. My own three indoor kitties had plenty of food, water, treats and anything else that the local pet store could provide. My older "girl," Maggie, who was my inspiration for the series of Magnificat books I had been writing for the last twenty years, had a choice of at least ten different things to eat daily, half of which she left. I hurried into my room and scooped up the left-over food before sliding outside into the bitter cold of an Ohio winter to leave the food remains, of which there were considerable, into the paws of the strays.

I knew where they had come from. In our neighborhood many people were losing their mortgages and being bitter, they dumped their pets before packing up and moving on to hopefully find jobs and careers elsewhere. These animals, dogs, cats, a parrot and even a gerbil haunted the old neighborhood as residents like myself, feeling sorry left tidbits for them to eat.

I watched over the next weeks and learned about some of these animals who were no longer loved or cared for. An older kitty, a tiger with a bad eye, seemed to be the leader; with his ear tipped I knew he had come from a shelter and was now neutered. I called him Bitty Tiger since he resembled my Bitty Kitty who had passed away five years previously and was buried at our local pet cemetery. The younger females loved Bitty Tiger but fortunately he was neutered. This was not true of the others in the group and four fresh litters of kittens were born the following spring.

Where do they go, I wondered to myself. The cats, Bitty Tiger, a little gray female I named Gray

Lady who had three beautiful kittens in the spring, several snowy white babies, Snowball and Snowflake, numerous black and white youngsters that I named Peanut, Pudding and Prudance. There was an adult, beautiful black cat who was shy and violently afraid of people and carefully watched my coming and going as he ate kitty chow out of one of the numerous bowls I had on my front porch.

After talking to the neighborhood grapevine, I realized that others in the area knew of the kitties plight. One older man had opened his barn, filled it with straw and hay, another lady had a heated garage which was left open to provide a warm place during the frigid nights, a third had a family of black cats that had been taken in over the years. As I watched the little troop gulp down the food that I placed outside, I knew that my house would be the one where these little cast-off souls would find a decent meal to eat, possibly the only one they had all day.

As time went one and I saw the cats as they came and went I noticed various things. One kitten rode on my back car bumper down to the end of the street. After jumping off, he found a home when he appeared on a doorstep. I frequented our local pet store and noted that some of "my" strays on display were being sponsored by the local animal organization Forever Friends. I later learned that some kind soul was taking them to the animal organization to be spayed or neutered and hopefully then to find homes.

The strays continued to eat on my porch as winter faded into spring and several new batches of kittens appeared. Gray Lady had three adorable babies, Grayling and his two siblings, while the all white kittens continued to roam. A nasty accident occurred when one fell while climbing our tree in the backyard while another was hit on a nearby busy street. Yet they survived in spite of the eagles and hawks from the local national park and the coyotes that roamed the area.

On one recent visit to the pet store, I noted two snow white kittens, obviously siblings of Snowball and Snowflake, who were domesticated and looking for a home along with four other black and white kittens, also seeking homes. They were no longer feral and wild, but peered at me cautiously and even hopefully out of their cages. They were ready to move on into the second of their nine lives thanks to the strangers who had taken them in and were helping to find forever homes.

The holiday season was coming and I knew that many potential adopters haunted the pet store in the weeks leading up to Thanksgiving and Christmas. I thought not only of the kitties but of all the people who had played a part in getting them here, where others could see, admire and then hopefully take them home.

"God bless them every one," I murmured aloud, referring not only to the cats, and people who were aiding them but the Lord above, who had given us all a chance to display true charity and love to those who needed it so badly.

The Purfect Pet

"So you're going to get a pet," my best friend, Morgan gushed at me over the telephone. "Tell me, Chloe, what sort of pet will it be?"

"Talk to you later," I mumbled. "My mother and I are on our way to the pet shop right now to see what they have."

I hung up the receiver and raced after my mother out of the apartment to our car. I was excited; my first pet and it was going to be fantastic! We drove rapidly to the Pet Place, where my mother spoke to the gray-haired owner. "We have an apartment," she murmured, "so it's going to have to be a small, quiet pet. Very quiet, because we have neighbors and a landlady."

"How about a dog?" the gray-haired owner offered.

"Dogs bark," my mother frowned thoughtfully.

"A small dog," the owner persisted, and brought out a long-eared puppy. "Half beagle. An ideal companion."

I held out my hand. The puppy came over and licked my fingers. "I like him."

My mother smiled and reached for her purse. Moments later she, I, and the puppy were back on the street headed for the apartment.

"What a lovely little dog," Morgan cooed when she stopped by after school. My puppy bounded after a ball in our family room. "What are you going to call him?"

"I haven't decided yet," I answered, moving to pick up the ball.

"Nice puppy," Morgan purred.

"Gurrrrr," said my puppy. A silence followed; then I heard a ripping noise and a shriek from my friend.

"What happened?"I cried, turning back to her.

'Look at my skirt!" Morgan wailed, sticking her hand through a newly-made hole. "My new Hannah Montana!"

"Gurrrr," said my puppy, attacking a red scrap of material lying on the rug.

"No luck?" asked the pet store owner the next day as my mother and I presented ourselves at the Pet Place with the puppy. "Surely the puppy didn't bite?"

"Just chewed. How about a nice cat?" my mother queried.

"Here's the ticket." He replaced the puppy with a green-eyed Burmese cat. "She doesn't bite or chew."

"Great." My mother watched the kitten chase after a piece of string I dangled under her nose.

She turned and we started out of the store, Green-Eyes tucked under my arm.

"You're sure about this one, aren't you?" Morgan of the defunct red skirt asked as she eyed my new pet nervously later the next day.

"Positive. She eats, sleeps, and plays. Doesn't bite and doesn't chew."

Morgan gushed, "Nice kitty, nice kitty."

I smiled. They would be friends for life. Then I heard a sudden, unexpected yell from Morgan.

"Look what she's done!" My friend hopped on one foot, her socks hanging in shreds. "She used my leg for a scratching post!"

Kitty sat in the middle of the floor, purring delightedly.

"More trouble?" asked the pet shop owner the following day as my mother and I presented ourselves with Kitty at his door.

"I need another replacement. No chewing or clawing. And this time I've got to have the right pet. An old college friend of my husband's is stopping in for dinner tonight!"

"I have the perfect animal." He disappeared and then returned, holding a yellow parakeet in a cage. "He's so tame, you can even let him fly alone around your apartment!"

I held out my hand. "I hope this one is O.K. I really liked my puppy and kitten."

My mother and I returned to our car.

That night over dinner, my father's college friend commented on Birdie. "Nice pet," he stated.
"We got him just this morning." My mother cast an eye upon Birdie, overlooking us from the top of a bookcase.
"More soup, Sir?" my father inquired.
He never did get an answer. As though on cue, Birdie swooped downward, claws unfurled, to snatch at the hair on the Professor's head. Fortunately, it was not permanently attached.
"My toupee!" gasped the Professor.
"Drop it Birdie!" I ordered.
"Cheep, cheep," said Birdie from his perch on the bookcase.
"What, back again?" inquired the pet store owner the next day as my father and I presented ourselves with Birdie on his doorstep.
"My dinner turned into a disaster," my father moaned, thinking of the unkind words of the evening before.
"He didn't like the main course?"

"We never got past the soup!"
"You're going to need another pet. We aim to please. How about some nice fish?"
I sadly held out my hand to Birdie to say goodbye. I was losing another friend! My father

watched me silently and then turned back to the pet store owner.

"Actually my wife and I have been thinking about the situation. And, we've decided there are no perfect pets. Just like there are no perfect people or anything else. But we may not be living in the apartment much longer anyway. I got a raise today, and my wife and I have decided to move into a small house...so, we'll take those fish and Chloe's puppy, kitten and Birdie back, too. With our own home, it doesn't matter that our pets aren't perfect. And we'll have room for them all!"

And that's just what we did!

A Shelter Called Kitten Krazy

Wendy Mirrotto has been called "that crazy cat lady" since she has found homes for 5000 cats and kittens over the last fourteen years after founding a shelter in Medina. The shelter was started in Mirrotto's garage and has been extended to a 4000 foot building. A black kitten called Hope was the 5000th feline to find a happy home.

Wendy began her career volunteering at an animal shelter in Parma; when she moved to Medina there was no such place available for cats so Kitten Krazy, Inc. was born. The animals are unwanted and are left wherever or are just dumped out onto the street and have nowhere to go. Volunteers also foster cats until homes are found; these fosters include people from the Grafton Correctional Institution and the Ohio Department of Rehabilitation. Mirrotto reports that the cats and kittens are adoptable after being frequently handled by the fosters since they are far more used to humans than previously which is a definite plus. A quick fix and spay program was also founded at the same time as Kitten Krazy, which boasts its 50,000th surgery. Both of these aids help unwanted cats find homes. The organizations rely on donations and fundraisers for monetary support.

<u>Ranching Alpaca Style</u>

The soft, dewy eyes peek into my face as the alpaca itches closer in friendship. I am visiting an alpaca farm and I am enchanted with these fuzzy creatures with their peaceful, doelike eyes and the warm fleece, that makes them so profitable to raise on ranches and farms just like Coffee Pot Farm in Sherrodsville, Ohio.

Alpaca Ranching. I had never heard of such a thing. Cows, horses, ponies, even mules perhaps. Yet alpaca ranching has spread throughout the United States with almost every state being represented in the AOBA, the Alpaca Owners and Breeders Association. In addition, it is not that hard to get started!

Alpacas were known as far back in history as the ancient Incas of South American in Peru. The fuzzy animals were domesticated over six-thousand years ago; the fibers from the alpaca fleece were so highly regarded that only Inca kings were permitted to wear these beautiful garments.

Ultimately, alpacas were brought to America, where an entire industry was born. These gentle animals became popular livestock additions; besides their almost comical dispositions, they are easy to care for and need a minimum of land on which to roam. Because they are hardy though expensive (one animal can cost hundreds or tens of thousands of dollars), alpacas are bred for sale. Dams (mothers) can be mated to males (sires) to produce crias (babies). The young can be sold or kept for their fleece and because alpacas are social animals with others of their kind, the more dams in the herd, the faster a business will grow.

Alpacas are related to camels and llamas, all members of the Camelid family, only much smaller and friendlier, which is one thing that makes them popular. The average alpaca can live for twenty-five years, producing young crias every year. There are over twenty different shades of color for the alpacas' fleece- white, black, brown and grey. Ninety percent of these animals are Huacaya alpacas; they look like fuzzy, adorable little bears and can yield as much as ten pounds of valuable fiber per year. This fiber is far superior to sheep wool for both softness and warmth and is not inclined to be "scratchy".

Alpacas come from South America and there is a ranch, the Accoyo Ranch in Peru, whose owners selectively breed the crème de la crème of these intelligent animals and produce the finest of fleece, which is hypo allergenic, another important consideration.

These popular alpacas have become investment opportunities for a wide variety of people. Bankers, doctors, farmers, ranchers, and retirees are all owners who enjoy the animals and the investment opportunities the alpaca offers. Small amounts of land, as little as one acre, are more than sufficient for a small herd. Cost is minimal aside from grain, hay, water, vitamins and barn cleaning. Since alpacas prefer to remain outside, barns can be minimal and only necessary in a harsh climate and because the alpaca are relatively small, it costs less to feed them then it does a large dog!

Because alpacas are also good with children, they make excellent pets and are such low maintenance animals that breeding them is a joy. Because their fleece is so highly-prized for everything from sweaters to slippers, they literally pay for themselves. The original price for a good animal is high and as such insurance must be carried, but the long term value of the alpacas far outweigh the original investment. Plus the animals adapt easily to a variety of circumstances, travel well and are calm with a quiet disposition. All of these reasons have lured more and more people to the alpaca; many are discovering the animal and are becoming acquainted for the first time.

For finding a long time friend or for a rewarding career that seems to be definitely on the upswing, or just dealing with enchanting, almost childlike animals that make good friends, alpaca farming is a career to consider.

Angel-Talkers

My Week-Week (Miss Sinbad) was a "talker". Part Siamese, but almost entirely black, she had been a rescue from a horse barn east of Cleveland, Ohio. I'd watched her and the other dozen or so kittens from the day I'd first spotted her when she'd gotten a glancing blow from a horse and limped around painfully. It was after that I took her home. Week-Week lived with me until she passed away twelve years later from a massive stroke.

My "talker" was gone. The house seemed so much quieter regardless of the fact that we had three other kitties. Munchkin, her buddy, missed her dreadfully. Then I heard about Maggie.

Maggie and dozens of other cats were going to be euthanized because of a terrible situation down in Akron, Ohio. A friend from Paws & Prayers Animal Organization brought her over when she'd heard I was searching for a black kitten. Maggie had worms and parasites from living out on the street. I looked at her and knew she would go home with me.

Today Maggie devotedly sleeps with me at night and plays happily with our other three rescue cats. She looks so much like Week-Week that sometimes I think she has returned to me, and I am so happy to have known them both.

From Alaska to Ohio: A Hero Named Balto Comes Home

One of the most renown hero dogs in the history of America was that of Balto, an Alaskan sled dog, who had ties to the State of Ohio. Balto's history was complicated and was deeply connected to the State of Alaska, specifically the city of Nome. Interest in the state had blossomed toward the end of the 1800's when gold was discovered in the city in 1898. This triggered a massive gold rush to the town located on the Seward Peninsula. Twenty thousand people overran the region inside of a few short months. Unfortunately for Nome, the gold was quickly panned out; people departed and the population shrunk to 1400 persons. Nome was hardly a traveler's delight; the cold, ice and frozen temperatures kept it isolated for seven months out of the year. The nearest post of civilization was the town of Nenana, 650 miles distant, which boasted of a railroad. Besides this, there was a radio telegraph; mail was carried by dog teams from

Anchorage in the south to Nome in the north. This route was later called the "Iditerod Trail" where a well-known race with dog teams and mushers is run yearly. It began in 1973.

In 1925 an emergency occurred in Nome and the radio signal was activated. The message "we have an outbreak of diphtheria" sent hearts pounding; this deadly disease of the time could be fatal and was in an area covered with snow and ice. The local Native American Inuit tribe was particularly susceptible to this contagious outbreak which affected the lungs and breathing. The message was fortunately received in Seattle and generated this response "Fresh serum available here" and only required a plane on standby to transport the serum to Nome. Disaster struck since the plane was unable to fly due to the cold. A frantic message from Anchorage asking for dog teams to transport the serum from Nenana, the end of the railroad line and on to Nome was broadcast. There was a quick response as the outbreak of diphtheria killed three children by the following day. A number of mushers and dog teams assembled to transport the serum to Nome. On January 27, 1925 "Wild Bill" Shannon took the medicine from the train and started west in minus 50 degree weather; part of his journey was also made in the dark. After 52 miles "Wild Bill" connected with Edgar Kalland who mushed onward; over a dozen mushers and their dogs participated in the "Great Race of

Mercy" in horrific conditions where the stouthearted dogs were freezing to death on their feet in drifts of snow over four feet high.

Ultimately the serum was passed to Gunnar Kaasen and his outstanding team of dogs led by Balto. This outstanding team survived an overturned sled and made it into Nome on February 2nd, setting a record for speed and making the team heroes throughout the lower United States.

The publicity of this outstanding feat caught the attention of Hollywood; a producer leased Balto to make a movie of this "Serum Race". The dog and Kassen were transported to Mt. Rainier in Washington State to star in a short-subject film "Balto's Race to Nome".

Balto and musher Kaasen became well-known throughout the United States after their successful endeavor in Alaska. Frederick Roth sculpted a statue of the dog for Central Park in New York City; at the first showing in 1925 Balto journeyed to NYC and was a spectator at the event. The inscription on the statue was noteworthy:

"Dedicated to the indomitable spirit of the sled dogs that relayed antitoxin six hundred miles over rough ice, across treacherous waters, through Arctic blizzards from Nenana to the relief of stricken Nome in the Winter of 1925.

Endurance Fidelity Intelligence"

Unfortunately Hollywood producer Sol Lesser and Kassen had a serious salary dispute. This ended with Kassen and the dogs being involved in a vaudeville act for the next two years. By this time Kassen and Balto were "old news"; Kassen returned to Nome and the dogs were put on display. Fortunately, they were spotted by George Kimble, a Cleveland businessman visiting in Los Angeles, who was appalled at the treatment the hero dogs were receiving. He struck a deal to buy Balto for $2000, but then needed to raise the money to save the dog's life. In this "race to save Balto", Kimble established a Balto Fund while radio broadcasters everywhere asked for donations. The local Cleveland paper, the "Plain Dealer", carried the story; school children, factory workers and everyone else opened their pockets to save the dogs. The Western Reserve Kennel Club added monies and in ten days the $2000 had been collected. Balto and the other huskies were coming home to Cleveland!

In honor of this event, a huge parade was held in Cleveland's Public Square. The dogs were then moved to their new home, the Brookside Zoo. Public interest remained high as over 15,000 people from all over Ohio and neighboring states visited the huskies in a single day! The dogs happily lived out their lives here, honored and loved by everyone.

Balto lived for fourteen years; his remains were mounted by The Cleveland Museum of Natural History. His story does not stop there; his legacy and heroic acts have been recorded by the museum for future generations to honor him. A special exhibition to honor the dog was proposed by the Anchorage Museum of History and Art in 1996.

School children from Alaska requested that the Cleveland Museum return Balto permanently to their state; they were supported in this endeavor by the Alaska State Legislature. The dispute was settled by the Cleveland Museum who felt that the dog's permanent home should be in Ohio. Regardless, the mounted Balto was sent for five months to the Anchorage Museum. A Cleveland guard went with the display with Balto mounted inside for the trip. The "Balto returns to Alaska" exhibit attracted a huge crowd of 65,000 people until he came home to Cleveland in 1999.

The dog was immortalized in several movies including an animated film produced in 1995 with a voice-over by Kevin Bacon, a comic book, "North of the Yukon" in 1965 and a book <u>The Cruelist Miles</u> in 2003. There were also radical changes in Alaska itself; the region became a state in 1959. Modern conveniences were introduced including better planes no longer so affected by extreme weather, telephones, television and snowmobiles for travel; these made everyone more independent of the environment and made sled dogs almost obsolete. Some people including Dorothy Page and Joe Redington, Sr. believed the old ways and traditions needed to be recognized, hence the "serum run trail" became the route for a famous race, the Iditarod over 1049 miles of rough Alaskan territory, which is celebrated yearly. These recollections serve to keep alive the days of yesteryear when dogs like Balto and the mushers who drove them helped settle the Alaskan wilderness and conquer this land far to the North.

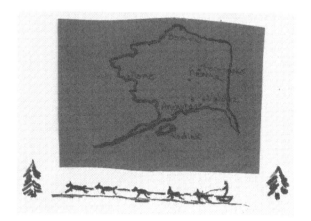

Kitty Tails II

That Groundhog Goofs Again

Now that the warm weather has officially arrived, people can stop lambasting the poor groundhog who said the weather was going to break early in 2013. Indeed, a prosecutor in Butler County, Ohio, has just criticized Punxsutawney Phil, Pennsylvania's most famous forecaster, for his disastrous prediction of an early spring. But should Ohioans really be annoyed? The little rodent only has a 39% success rate, higher than most weathermen with all their fancy gadgets, and never claimed, unless people can understand groundhogese, that he was a forecaster at all!

The legend surrounding this little animal and his forecasts goes back to European folklore and was brought to this country by German and Amish immigrants, who established a large settlement in Holmes County and in Middlefield, east of Cleveland. According to legend, if the groundhog sees his shadow on February 2nd, he becomes frightened and returns to his burrow. This indicates that there will be six more weeks of winter weather. If the groundhog doesn't see his shadow, he moves confidently away from his burrow since winter will end early for the year.

Groundhogs are unique animals. Belonging to the rodent family, they are also called woodchucks, land beavers, or marmots. Being the biggest in the family, groundhogs can weigh as much as 31 pounds, have thick claws and live by eating fruits, vegetables, and wild plants including grasses.

Groundhogs store excessive body fat for their hibernation each year, usually in tunnels or burrows from October to March, except for February 2nd, when they appear on Groundhog Day, their moment of fame, to see or not to see their shadow. They are noteworthy since they catch millions of insects each year that eat farm crops; for this reason they are important in agricultural states such as Ohio.

The groundhog is most commonly found in the north central region of the United States. Numerous areas have their own weather prognosticators including Staten Island Chuck (New York), General Beauregard Lee (Georgia), Balzac Billy (Alberta, Canada), Wiarton Willie (Ontario, Canada), Buckeye Chuck and Strasburg Sam (Ohio) and the most famous, Punxsutawney Phil. Phil, who has made his predictions from Punxsutawney in Western Pennsylvania since at least 1886, is featured yearly on television news and starred in his own movie, "Groundhog Day" along with Bill Murray.

Ohio's two weather forecasters are also achieving increasing notoriety; Buckeye Chuck, whose home is in Marion, Ohio and Strasburg Sam from the town of the same name located in Amish country of Holmes County. Sam, the latest addition to weather forecasting groundhogs, is free roaming; he is far more likely to appear when food is offered than when there are clouds or the sky is clear. Sam reigns in a scenic village of 2600 people in an area a little over one mile square. He sleeps throughout the winter and heavy rainy seasons and appears when the weather is milder and far more pleasant. Strasburg is in the center of the largest Amish community in the world; the area is filled with friendly people and farms that resemble Currier and Ives prints, ideal for sightseeing after Sam has made his prediction for the year.

Named Ohio's official weather forecaster, Buckeye Chuck resides in Marion, Ohio, not far from Columbus. On February 2, 2013, Chuck exited his warm burrow at 7:39 a.m., saw the snow and overcast skies and dived back inside his home after not seeing his famous shadow. His cheering crowd of approximately 200 individuals shouted loudly before decamping to warmer (the temperature was about 14 degrees) climes. Buckeye Chuck and Punxsutawney Phil agreed that it was going to be an early spring.

Forecasting on the Christian holiday of Candlemas in olden times, human weather forecasters admit that 2013 would be an almost impossible year to accurately predict. Temperatures ranged from a high of 67 degrees in the Columbus area, where Buckeye Chuck dwells to a complete about face by the end of the week with buffeting winds causing a cold, chilling climate.

The winter of 2012 was far easier to forecast because temperatures were warmer and well above average, with a distinct lack of snow in the Ohio (midwest area). Regardless of the cold, Chuck had his supporters in 2013; specifically 20 Scouts who camped overnight, ate Spam sandwiches that according to tall tales contain groundhog, and braved the cold to watch Chuck make his famous forecast. Regardless of the gloomy day, the Scouts did have a great time.

Buckeye Chuck has been making his forecasts since the mid-1970's; the Ohio legislature officially recognized him as Ohio's forecaster in 1979. Groundhogs living in the wild survive on average of only two years while those kept inside average ten or more years. Adding to Chuck's legendary prowess are those who contend he has survived for thirty years and is still going strong!

A similar claim has been made by those harboring Punxsutawney Phil in a heated library in Pennsylvania when the groundhog is not working on his famous one-day-per year schedule. Although the celebration is more formal as the mayor, who opens the ceremony with the words "All hail groundhog supremacy" and dignitaries dressed in top hats and tails at Gobbler's Knob outside of the town, end results have been remarkably similar between the two animals. As people go on their way to celebrate Groundhog Day at the "Groundhog Hop" with food and great drink, the weather forecaster returns to his inside burrow and goes back to sleep to wait for warmer days.

Each weather predictor has his own unique traits and his own "fan club" of devotees. Staten Island Chuck of New York, who lives in the local zoo, dwells in a tiny log cabin with his name above the door. Mayor Bloomberg, who was bitten by Chuck in 2009 after interrupting the groundhog's sleep, has declined to officiate or even attend another Groundhog Day; a city council speaker has substituted for him ever since! General Beauregard Lee dwells at the Yellow River Game Ranch, located outside of Atlanta, Georgia. The groundhog holds honorary doctorates from Georgia State University and the University of Georgia as a "Doctor of Southern Groundology" and "Doctor of Weather Prognostication"; his success rate is a whopping 94%. His one and only disaster was in 1993 when Georgia suffered through the "Storm of the Century" after General Lee forecast an early spring.

And what's ahead for future forecasters on the part of the furry little groundhog? That remains to be seen as thousands flood Marion, Ohio, Punxsutawney, Pennsylvania, and Staten Island, New York where the groundhog reigns supreme in his place of glory one day each year.

An Expedition to the Far North

It was an adventure of a lifetime that occurred over thirty years ago but which will never be forgotten. My mother and I traveled to Prince Edward Island where we stayed overnight. The following day we boarded a helicopter and flew out over the ice-coated sea to view one of the most amazing of nature's shows. Every March the baby harp seals are born on the ice floes and develop into adults under their mother's guidance. Tourists had been venturing out over the ice to view this amazing phenomenon of nature, the tiny, newly born babies which were surprisingly tame for wild animals. Now it was our turn to view these little white seals on an adventure of a lifetime.

The helicopter traveled carefully over the grey flecked sea until we saw a huge ice floe beneath us. The pilot set the helicopter down cautiously and we disembarked to wander over the ice for a close up view of the tiny white babies in front of us. I carefully held out my hand to pet one of the little seals.

It seemed to be unafraid of the tourists taking pictures and filming the adventure for viewing back home. I was approached by a lady from a Cleveland area television station who asked politely if I would mind her taking some film of me meeting the seals for the first time. I told her to go ahead as I knelt down on the ice and continued to pet the tiny white animal.

Mother seal stayed close but surprisingly didn't do anything to interfere; perhaps she knew that we meant no harm but only came to look, unlike the seal hunters who also came in the spring.

I noted a large hole in the blue-green ice through which the mother could disappear. The little ones were virtually helpless until their swimming skills were developed; until then they lived on the ice. Over 250,000 of the mothers traveled from Greenland to the St. Lawrence Gulf every year to bear their young.

We traveled back to our hotel at the end of the day before flying home. Because of the extreme interest of wildlife conservationists like myself, the baby seals eventually were protected from the hunters. I discovered that my friend with the movie camera broadcast my meeting with the seals; my friends at work thrilled to see me on television as they got to view firsthand what I did on my vacation. They were quite impressed to have a "movie star" working in their midst as my adventure of a lifetime was recorded for all posterity to view.

Pickle Bill's Restaurant: a Food and Animal Lover's Delight

For a unique sailing and dining experience, sail your boat from Lake Erie upstream to Grand River, Ohio, to a "drive-in boat restaurant" called Pickle Bill's (the traditional landlubbers way by car is possible, but isn't nearly as much fun!). At this one-of-a-kind restaurant, you can eat tasty seafood, steaks and more at a reasonable price or view museum items such as an old-time scuba suit (typical of the Disney movie *Twenty Thousand Leagues under the Sea*) up close. Perhaps dining on a floating pavilion in the middle of a river after boaters disembark for a marvelous lunch or dinner is more up your alley. Or if you are an animal person, feeding gulls, ducks and geese who come calling and are so close they will almost take bread from your hand brings joy to your heart. Then Pickle Bill's located on the Grand River, is the place for you!

Pickle Bill's is a restaurant complete with party rooms and a gift shop but it is also so much more.

Ship paraphernalia are displayed throughout the establishment along with ship figureheads, a stuffed alligator (fake), and art work from different eras in history. Even the bathrooms are different since they remind one of the Art Deco days of long ago. Needless to say, the restaurant has something to appeal to every taste along with dining inside with heat and air conditioning, outside (on a patio overlooking the river), or in the pavilion (on a floating platform on the Grand River itself).

This floating platform gives visitors a close up view of the craft plying the waterway as well as the wildlife in the area besides the feeling of literally sitting in the middle of the channel. Aside from the gulls and small sparrows there are the beautiful Canada geese, who swim around the platform begging for handouts from the diners as they enjoy the tasty food.

There are also a wide variety of boats to view, many coming from the nearby marinas on the Grand River as they sail out to Lake Erie. Friendly boaters wave and frequently pull their craft into the docks adjacent to the restaurant, stopping for a drink or a meal before continuing their journey out into the lake.

A note about the history of this unique establishment: this is the second Pickle Bill's Restaurant. The first, founded by Gerald Gilson Powell, was located in the Cleveland flats on Old River Road on the Cuyahoga River. The name Pickle Bill's stemmed from Mr. Powell's admiration of W.(William) C. Fields, an actor and comedian in the black-and-white era of feature films during the Great Depression. The main character was noted for being "pickled" in the films, hence the transfer of the name to Pickle Bill's Restaurant.

The establishment moved to its current location on River Street in 1982. Additional rooms for increased seating capacity were added, along with such displayed treasures as the doors from the Terminal Tower in Cleveland, a Pilot House from the freighter "Austin", plus "the Barge", a floating bar/dock in the middle of the Grand River. Unfortunately, this second version of Pickle Bill's was destroyed by fire in 1998. In spite of the disaster, the owner refused to let the restaurant die; he rebuilt and reopened in 2000. His faith was rewarded since Pickle Bill's thrives today, a truly unique place that both adults and children can enjoy.

Falkland Islands Odessey

"Peat?" I mumbled aloud. Like in Ireland? And the local inhabitants used it for fuel?

I stared at the greenish brown island in front of me. The westerly wind blasted across the water in the harbor below, making choppy, frothy waves across the bay. Out on the water, the cruise ship from which I had disembarked waited patiently. The launch that had brought passengers ashore had returned to the ship. I could barely see the crew waiting for the next group of tourists to gather and leave the ship for their visit to Port Stanley, capital city of the Falkland Islands.

I had known very little about the Falkland Archipelago first hand. An article in a geography book pinpointed the islands as being in the South Atlantic approximately three hundred and fifty miles off the coast of Argentina. The islands had been colonized first by the Dutch, then by the English, the French and finally the Spanish. Abandoned by Spain, the area was eventually resettled by the English. Here, thousands of miles from the "mother country", were islands whose natives spoke English, had afternoon tea, and used peat for fuel!

The local guide, whose name was Alan, had met us at the landing dock. He smiled broadly, spoke with a delightful English accent and brought our group of tourists to this peat field (not bog). Here the local residents had their sections staked out to dig peat.

"But what keeps them from digging all of it out and then not having any fuel?" a member of the group wondered aloud.

"It's government regulated. Only nobody will be digging today. This is Sunday. With the seasons being reversed, it is our spring even though the month is December."

I nodded as I pulled up the collar of my winter coat. The seasons were opposite, south of the Equator. I wondered how cold it actually got as I noticed several of my companions shivering in light jackets. If this were spring, how cold did it get over the winter?

"It's rather balmy today, actually," Alan seemed to know what tourists were thinking. "We don't have extremes in weather. No piles of snow and no hundred degrees. Of course, the wind off the water can be a little brisk. And we do have serious gale weather here. Many ships are lying in the bay that never made it back to port. Shipwrecked they were."

He paused and then waved an arm expansively. "Go and look at the peat if you'd like to. Just don't go beyond the edges of the fields."

I turned back. "Because we'd be trespassing?"

"No. We're all friends here. Because of the mines."

I must have looked blank so he explained.

"The war in 1982 with Argentina. When Port Stanley was attacked and occupied for two months, the Argentinians mined the fields and beaches."

"And the mines haven't been removed?"

"No. Still there. Just don't wander any place off limits. The birds are safe, but anything much heavier..."

"Right," I muttered. I took a look at the peat; it was dried out and rather hard. I very carefully didn't venture beyond the peat patch, although I noticed petrels, geese, finch and an albatross settling comfortably in the nearby field.

Alan beckoned us back to the bus. On the way toward town, we stopped at a totem pole and mileage indicator. Of course all of us had to have our pictures taken at this tourist sight.

After, we again clamored aboard the bus. I noted here that the road was surprisingly good. Obviously the local citizens cared a great deal about the island. This was borne out as the bus proceeded through the capital with its buildings capped by metal roofs.

Port Stanley is a brightly-colored, well-laid out miniature town, neat and well-kept, with trimmed, fenced yards. I could see the spire of the Christian Anglican church dominating the skyline in the center. The bus drove past a main square decorated with a whalebone arch. Whales had at one time been central to the island's economy. Now of course the tourists were very important along with raising sheep on the farms.

And why did the tourists come?

"The wildlife," our guide told us."'The birds, in part. But there are rockhopper penguins and seals across the bay on the outer island."

My gaze wandered from Alan down the main street, Ross Road. I noted several small, well-kept hotels. The Upland Goose struck my eye. This would be a good place to relax and enjoy nature.

The bus halted by a brown wooden building complete with a metal roof known as Britannia House. It was the Museum of the Falkland Islands. Shepherding us inside, Alan left the group to wander back through Falkland history, which was dominated by the Argentinian invasion during the Falkland War in the 1980's.

The islanders, of course, had suffered first-hand under the Argentinian occupation before being liberated by English forces two months later. "But many people still have nightmares about it," the curator of the museum, Mr. John Smith, mentioned.

I could see why. Peaceful was the word that came to my mind as I looked around outside the museum. I spotted a house with a glassed in garden porch. It was trimmed with flowers and a couch where a small girl slept. I couldn't imagine this small group of islands being invaded but it had happened.

The bus left us off close to the central square, where everyone dispersed to wander on their own before taking the launch back to the ship.

I ambled up the main street of the town, past the Upland Goose Hotel and the ornately decorated Anglican Church.

Farther along past gardens of blooming yellow flowers was a second, smaller church, St. Mary's, just before Ross Road petered out. I circled and made my way back into the center of town.

Three of the local inhabitants waved as I strolled down the main street. The wind now blew at my back, pushing me along as I passed more small, well-kept yards with children playing in the rear. A tiger cat sidled over, friendly, yet curious. Farther down the street, I could see a local handicraft store selling woolens and souvenirs that seemed to be doing a brisk business. Close by was a grocery also busy with tourists and locals alike.

Returning to the wharf, I spotted part of our group in a brightly-painted shop by the pier. Within was everything from pins to tee-shirts to wildlife pictures from Port Stanley in the Falkland Islands. Farther along, by the water's edge, was a kiosk selling more tee-shirts with the locals serving free hot tea to the tourists.

The wind was kicking the water up in little angry swirls as I boarded the launch to return to the cruise ship. The freshness of Port Stanley lingered with me...the sea air, the fragrance of the flowers, the quietness and peace. Throughout my ramblings, the charm of this English town seemingly transported onto an island in the South Atlantic remained with me. I would remember the orderliness, neatness, and friendliness of the people. Taking a last look as I boarded the launch,

I spotted the tiger cat from my earlier ramblings. She had been joined by her black mate, who, I imagined, bid me farewell as the launch pulled away from the jetty toward the ship.

"Come back again," I imagined her to say.

"I plan to," I said aloud and smiled.

A Caregiving Kitty

Her name is Libby, she is seven years old and is a "caregiving kitty" to twelve year old Cashew who is deaf and blind. Libby leads her doggie soul mate around every day to food, water and a bed where they sleep together at night. They are apart only when Cashew goes out for a walk with his owner on the streets of Pennsylvania. The dog and cat are devoted to each other and would be so alone if separated. Libby shows extreme animal love all day every day and has done so for years to her dearest friend; they love each other dearly and are lucky to have one another.

Blackwood's Angel

I look around the room. My eyes wander up and down, up and down and I see her sitting by the door; the black cat with the white blaze on her forehead. She has befriended me but I know not why since I am a virtual prisoner with no hope of escape. I pull my eyes away and study the crack in the ceiling for perhaps the hundredth time; it meanders along like a river on a map and then dissolves into nothing. White, all white. Floor, ceiling, walls with windows that are covered over. The sunlight filters through making odd little speckles on the table near me. I sit there and wait. For what, I am not sure…Whatever. It will be about the money likely as not.

Then the door opens and he comes in, tall, good-natured, smiling. Dressed in a white coat. More white. I frown as I think about him. Across his pocket is a plastic name tag that says FRAZIER in bold, black letters. A doctor no doubt. I wonder if he came again about the money. Money I had inherited when my aunt and uncle were killed in a car crash. Money which would not be mine if the man facing me could show that I am not mentally stable just like my cousin wants.

He sees my frown of course. Always. He is very astute that way. Very sensitive and he asks me about it straight off.

"You seem depressed today. Is it anything in particular, Mrs. Angel?" He puts a small tape recorder down on the table trying to be unobtrusive about it but I notice. I'm too smart for him as usual.

My eyes are drawn to the table. The tape inside the recorder goes round and round. I watch it, mesmerized.

"Mrs. Angel?"

I jump, startled. Then I realize that he has asked me a question. I respond with a question of my own.

"I've wondered something about you. Don't you ever frown? All you've ever done is smile since I first laid eyes on you. Smiling then, smiling now."

He seems disconcerted. I am delighted. Score one for me. I like him to feel as ill-at-ease as possible. The way he so often makes me feel. My mood brightens immediately.

The black cat moves from her position by the door as though sensing my change in mood. She crosses the room to snuggle up beside me. My hand strokes her automatically.

I see Frazier follow the cat with his eyes. He looks upset for a moment but then his smile returns almost as though it has been plastered onto his face with glue.

He tries unsuccessfully to answer my question. "No, of course I frown. I have problems just like anyone else." But he smiles when he says it. Even the cat can feel the insincerity in his voice and utters a low hiss. I sigh inwardly and decide to try a new tact.

"Tell me, what day is it? I saw a Christmas tree when I went downstairs earlier. Is it Christmas yet?"

Frazier looks relieved as though glad to get off the subject of his smiling. "No, not yet. Two more weeks. But everyone is putting the decorations up early this year."

"I saw the tree. It is such a pretty tree. Like that other one." Suddenly I have trouble swallowing. A beautiful tree, stories high, gleaming with multicolored lights. How long ago had I seen that tree?

"What tree are you remembering?"

I pull myself erect. "I don't want to talk about it any more. Just a tree." I cannot stop my mind from working or my mouth either, so it seems.

"I was young then. And pretty. Not like now."

It seems that the black cat can feel my extreme distress. She comes closer and snuggles next to me. Her eyes close.

"Calm yourself. There's no reason to be so upset. It will come back to you."

I bury my face in the cat's black hair. "I don't know. Will it?" I ask Frazier. As I turn to look at him the tears begin traveling in rivulets down my face. I rock faster and faster on my chair. The cat stares at me with wide, unblinking eyes as Frazier hands me a handkerchief soundlessly. Meanwhile the tape in the little recorder runs out and then stops.

It seems the cat has adopted me! I feel a streak of joy fill my soul; at least something living wants and desires my company. I have named her Blackwood. I am holding her close at my next meeting with Frazier.

"I've remembered!" I exclaim triumphantly. "About the tree and everything! It was at Christmas when my aunt and uncle died. In a car crash and they disinherited my cousin, Roger. And left their money to me!"

I thought back. Everything had changed for me then. I went to school, got a good job with the telephone company. But my cousin hated me! At the reading of the will he told me to spend the money wisely since I wouldn't have it too long!

"What are you thinking?" Frazier asks as I stop talking.

"My cousin. Roger. And my aunt and uncle. They died in an automobile crash. He was a mechanic. I always half thought that he'd..."

Frazier waited. "Done something to their car?"

I hold Blackwood closer. She purrs low in my ear. "Yes. They were his parents you know. They left him without a cent."

"Do you know why?"

I rock back and forth slowly in my chair. "I guess I thought they'd suspected him of trying to kill them. And..." I gulped, "I think I thought so too."

Suddenly Frazier closes his notebook with a pop. "Well, we'll leave it there for now." He rises suddenly and moves toward the door. Blackwood gives a low hiss and springs from my lap.

"You'll see me tomorrow, then? I've finally remembered! After all of this time." I speak triumphantly, sure that he must be happy for me too.

"Of course." But his voice somehow lacks conviction. He passes through the door.

Blackwood hesitates, then slithers outside too. She looks back, her eyes almost beseeching me to follow.

I hesitate. Oh, why not. I pull myself out of the chair and trail her down the steep stairs and outside.

The bright sunlight hits my eyes. Used to the semidarkness, I blink rapidly, then brush a hand across my face. When I pull my hand away I see them.

They are standing behind a group of mountain ash trees partially hidden from my view. Blackwood trots rapidly ahead of me, then looks back. I trail her behind the ash trees. I can't see the two men but I can hear their voices distinctly.

"She's remembered a part of what happened. The accident. And she suspects how it happened. I'd hoped..."

"It's just a matter of time until it all comes back. And she blabs to someone who will investigate and do something about it." I recognize the nasal tones of my cousin, Roger.

"So what are we going to do?" Frazier's voice holds a note of despair.

"The smart thing, of course. I'm coming back with you and we will take care of the whole problem here and now. My cousin Frances takes an overdose of a drug, goes to sleep and never wakes up again."

I hear the shock in Frazier's voice. "But I'm a doctor! I can't just..."

Roger laughs, a low vicious sound. "You're an unlicensed nothing and have been for years!" He draws a breath. "Don't worry. I'll give her the drug. All you need do is stay out of the way."

I hear the footsteps as the two men come closer to where Blackwood and I are hiding. I turn and move rapidly back to the hospital, dart up the stairs and stop on the balcony overlooking the first floor.

Suddenly I peer downward. Blackwood is no longer at my feet! She has remained on the first floor as the two men enter.

"What's that cat doing here again?" Frazier asks as he and Roger enter. I watched him aim a kick in her direction.

"Don't worry about her now. Let's get upstairs and take care of our little problem."

I lean my head back against the door. What can I do? I'm trapped! There is no place left for me to go!

I watch with horror as the men climb the stairs. Blackwood seems to have disappeared but then I spot her! She is hiding behind one of the two top steps blending in with the dark carpeting and almost impossible to see.

As Frazier and my cousin come closer they move to cross her path. Blackwood raises herself slightly, just enough for my cousin to catch his heel in her hair. He lets out a shout and grabs for Frazier's arm.

Unfortunately for him, the doctor has just moved forward and is off balance. The men cling together before they start falling, over and over, back down the steep staircase. I hear a nasty crunch of bone meeting hard flooring as they reach the bottom.

My cousin, Roger, is on the bottom but I'm not sure it would have mattered. I scramble to the balcony to watch as Blackwood extricates herself from the heap and moves toward the door.

I can see that she doesn't need to be frightened of the two men any longer. Nobody need be frightened of them any longer. My cousin's neck is bent at an odd angle; I don't need to be a doctor to know that it is broken. Frazier's head is bleeding, the red blood streaming down his face and saturating the collar of his shirt. He will not be going anywhere soon either.

I can feel the pounding in my head as I rock back and forth. Sweat begins to pour out of me, around my mouth, eyes and hands. Then I look down and see Blackwood staring at me.

I can almost feel the command. "Come," she is saying. I move back into my all white room, grab my purse and hurry down the steep stairs to follow her around the two men and out of the door.

Blackwood turns to peer at me before she leads us both away from the white sanitarium building and over toward the woods. I follow, my mind frozen with what has just occurred. Then it comes to me, I am no longer a prisoner! I am free. Nobody has seen the accident and the men may not even be found immediately. I will be long gone and far away when they are discovered and since there is nothing to connect me with their nasty fall...

Blackwood trots ahead of me toward the nearby wooded thicket. Where is she going? I realize suddenly that it doesn't matter; I trust her more than I ever trusted Frazier all the time I was in the hospital. The kitty will not lead me astray.

She turns and gives a loud "Meow!" as though telling me to hurry up. Perhaps she has people of her own somewhere and maybe they will help me now. After all, I am a wealthy woman and can certainly afford to pay them.

The sun breaks through the trees as I follow my little savior through the woods and out onto the nearby road. I trail along as she turns left. Wherever my kitty is taking me, I know suddenly that it will be a better tomorrow. More importantly with her at my side, the two of us will be just fine.

I smile to myself. The sun has come out and it is truly a wonderful, wonderful day.

Shadowland Pets

Susan wanted a rabbit. She wanted a fish and a cat and a dog, too.

"You can't have a pet," her mother told her. "We live in an apartment. No pets! It is the rule here. And besides, your father may lose his job. Pets cost money!"

"Just a fish?" Susan asked. "To be my friend. A fish in a bowl wouldn't cost so much. And I could work after school doing odd jobs at the grocery. It would help pay for fish food."

"But a fish is still a pet. And our landlord says no. We can't afford another place, Susan. It's the way things have to be."

Susan looked sadly after her mother as she left the room. But rules were rules.

Susan's grandfather had been sitting quietly in a rocker by the window. Now he approached his granddaughter.

"Why do you look so unhappy?" he asked Susan.

"I wanted a pet rabbit for Easter. Only...our landlord says 'No pets!' Not even a fish!"

"I'll show you a way to have as many pets as you want. And they won't cost you one cent!" her grandfather replied.

He walked over to a large lamp and turned it on. The light reflected shadows onto the wall. Her grandfather held up two fingers in his one hand, which he made into a fist. Then he waggled the "ears."

"And here," he finished, "is your cat and your dog!"

Susan watched the animals appear on the wall. Then she duplicated the movements her grandfather had made.

"Pets! Lots and lots of pets!"

"And they are free and can come to you any time you want. As often as you want. All you need is a bright light and an empty wall!"

"Thank you," Susan said, "for giving me my shadow pets for friends!"

Do you want "Shadow Pets" too? Here's how! Just follow these directions!

Cross hands at the wrist, fingers
closed tightly. Move hands up and
down for a bird in flight.

Make a fist with the hand, leaving the thumb
and index finger slightly extended. Stick
toothpicks between the fingers for whiskers.
With the second hand, hold two fingers be-

hind the head for a kitty!

Take one hand, fingers extended. The
second hand makes two fingers behind
the head. Move the thumb for a dog barking!
Extend just one hand and close the fingers
except for the thumb. Move the thumb to and fro.
You have a quacking duck.

Extend one hand with closed fingers. Place
the second hand with fingers spread on top
of the head. You will have a deer with antlers.

Extend one hand with a rapid waving
motion. Keep fingers and thumb tucked
tightly in. You will have a fish.

Make a fist with the thumb tucked into the hand.

153

The wrist should slant downward. Extend the index and second fingers of the other hand for the ears.

Have fun with these pets! No fuss, no mess and they are great friends who always agree with you! What could be better?

A Mouse Whose Name Was Mickey

It has been 90 years since the most famous mouse in history was introduced to American audiences. Celebrations of this historic event will be going on all year on television, in the newspaper, and other media outlets.

The mouse is Mickey Mouse who was created by Walt Disney when he was launching the Disney empire in 1928; the mouse was his first success story whose fame with adults and children alike grew over the years. Mickey's first sound cartoon was "Steamboat Willie"; he went on to star in 130 films. In the beginning, Disney voiced his famous mouse using a high falsetto tone. Mickey became serious competition to another cartoon character of the era, Felix the Cat. When Felix transitioned to a sound cartoon, he lost his popularity among children and adults who turned to Disney's mouse as a substitute.

Disney established his studio in California and produced the most successful animated cartoon film of all time "Snow White and the Seven Dwarfs." The popularity of this film firmly established Walt and his brother Roy in the Hollywood scene; with the profits the brothers built a home for their parents Elias and Ohioan Flora (Call). A tragic accident turned this time of success into a disaster when a gas leak caused Flora to succumb to asphyxiation; her son, Walt blamed himself for this event for the rest of his life. His mother's death caused the young man to avoid characters with mothers in his movies; some like Bambi lost their mothers and were forced to do without them, similar to the situation with the Disney brothers.

In spite of this accident, the brothers continued to prosper in Burbank where their studio was established. Mickey Mouse remained a prime permanent fixture as he successfully made the jump from short cartoon features to movies with "Fantasia". He also starred in his own comic strip which first debuted in 1930 and ran for forty-five years. Mickey had a girlfriend, Minnie Mouse, a dog Pluto, friends Goofy and Donald Duck and was known for being a nice guy. This most unusual character met tourists when Disney's parks were established. In 1978 Mickey was awarded a star on the Hollywood Walk of Fame, the first cartoon creation to have such an honor.

Marketing created "Mickey" items such as wrist watches beginning in 1930; these items were sold for $3.75. Almost half of the Disney revenues came from products with Mickey Mouse branded on their merchandise.

A Fieldmouse Like Mickey

Mickey was also the source for a popular television series in the late 1950's (1955-1958) "The Mickey Mouse Club" and was revived several times over the years; the talented mouse was featured in every episode. The program introduced a number of teen stars to American audiences the most famous of which was Annette Funicello who went on to become a major movie star. The cast wore mouse ears and were known by their title of Mouseketeers; the show was a variety program featuring singing, dancing and a serial. Although aimed at children, many adults became fans of the program which took them back to their youth and a more simple time in America.

Mickey Mouse garnered ten nominations for an Academy Award, winning the prestigious award once for an animated short film titled "Lend a Paw". His creator, Walt Disney was awarded an honorary Academy Award for created the most well-liked mouse in existence. Besides this Mickey was a Grand Marshal of the Tournament of Roses Parade in 2005 on New Year's Day.

Mickey Mouse has had a long and exciting career being a most unusual mouse. Many experts have praised his personality and his likeability. In 2018 his character is a 90 year old mouse making him very notable indeed! In the words of his creator, Walt Disney, "I only hope that we never lose sight of one thing- that it was all started by a mouse."

The Russian Troika

Back in the days of yesteryear, when Americans rode horses and drove buggies instead of driving cars and trucks, a Christmas tree was brought home by a horse- drawn sled. In Russia, by contrast, sledding was done by a team of three horses called a troika. The troika was used by the Russian people to drag heavy loads across the rough terrain. Horses were carefully trained to pull the sleighs with the center horse of the three trotting while the side animals proceeded at a gallop. All three animals had to be taught to work together, a time-consuming process of as long as ten years.

The Russians often had contests to see which animals could pull the sleds over the frozen tundra at the fastest speeds. The Orlov horses were bred especially for this purpose; when the horses worked together, the effect was so smooth as to be described as similar to a bird flying.

During the 1940's and 1950's, there was a "Cold War" of poor diplomatic relations between the

United States and the Soviet Union (Russia). Cyrus Eaton, an American businessman and cattle breeder, who was born in Nova Scotia, Canada, lived over forty years ago; Eaton felt that the two countries should try harder to get along. He sent the Soviet Union a prized shorthorn steer from his farm in Northfield, Ohio as a gift in 1959.

The Soviet Union responded by sending Eaton three beautiful white troika horses to pull sleighs. Eaton's effort for cooperation with the Soviets earned him the Lenin Peace Prize in 1960.

Eaton's three troika horses and sleigh were a familiar sight in the Northfield region for years. The horses lived in a pasture at Eaton's Acadia Farms and could be seen by visitors. The animals were a reminder that friendship and peace were possible with other peoples, who perhaps were not as different as previously thought.

Kitty Tails II

A Museum to Honor Ohioan Roy Rogers, King of the Cowboys

His real name was Leonard Slye but to three generations of adults and children he was known as Roy Rogers King of the Cowboys and his wonder horse, Trigger. Rogers had a relatively nondescript start in life; after being born in a tenement in Cincinnati, his family moved to a houseboat in Portsmouth, Ohio, and eventually settled in Duck Run on a farm. Here young Leonard learned many of the necessary skills of the cowboy such as horsemanship. He also learned how to sing and yodel before the family returned to Cincinnati where the father and son went to work in a shoe factory to supplement the family income.

A turning point was reached when father and son visited Len's sister in California and ended by packing up the family and moving there. Young Len found employment driving a gravel truck and later picking peaches. He joined a country music group, the Rocky Mountaineers; later formed his own group, Sons of the Pioneers, and became popular on the radio. Their songs were played across the country and the group signed a contract with Decca Records which brought increased publicity for their first song, "Tumbling Tumbleweeds".

Roger's voice brought him a small role in a Gene Autry movie; when Autry demanded more money in 1938 for his work there was a huge opening for another "singing cowboy" at Republic Pictures. Rogers won a contest and played the lead in a western "Under Western Stars". He soon became a box office star and went on to compete with Autry, ultimately winning the top box office position from 1939 to 1954. Rogers became a role model for children. His pictures were also made in "living color" while most others were in black and white during these years. Besides the movies, Rogers name appeared on a variety of other products including comic books and action figures; these collectables became gigantic marketing success stories and added to Roger's fame and popularity.

Many fans have wondered if there was serious competition between Roy Rogers and Gene Autry, the original "singing cowboy" during the years (1940-1960). Although the two men were rivals with each other, they were also friends. Rogers appeared in an early movie of Autry's before he became King of the Cowboys in 1938. Both men were successful television/movie stars who also recorded popular songs, many which have been retained to the present day. Autry's "Rudolph the Red-Nosed Reindeer" is still heard at Christmas time, being one of the favorite songs of all time while Rogers "Don't Fence Me In" and "Jingle Jangle Jingle" also are still popular songs. Both men had horses which had their own fan clubs, namely Trigger and Champion. Rogers was more focused on his family of nine children while Autry, who never had offspring, was more centered on business.

Rogers personal life was not always happy; he lost his wife to complications from childbirth when his son Roy, Jr. (Dusty) was born.

He met Dale Evans in 1944 when they played together in a movie; the two married and adopted five children after their daughter, Robin, died of the mumps. Evans and Rogers costarred on his very popular television series which made them a household name; she wrote the famous song "Happy Trails" with which they ended episodes of their television series. Roy Rogers licensed his name to the Marriott Corporation in 1968 and the Roy Rogers Restaurants were born. Rogers also operated a Hollywood production company during the years which produced his television series.

Almost as famous as Roy Rogers and Dale Evans was Trigger, Rogers' horse, who was born in 1932. Trigger played an important part in the Rogers' television show and became almost a family member to several generations of children.

The singing group that Rogers was associated with, Sons of the Pioneers, achieved stardom and became known coast-to-coast with over thirty recordings on Decca Records. They often were the musical backup group for Rogers' films and television show and appeared frequently with him over the years until his death in 1998. He was awarded a Golden Boot Award and he and his wife were inducted into the Western Performers Hall of Fame in 1976.

A museum dedicated to Rogers was opened in Branson, Missouri in 2003. Unfortunately, the museum failed and Dusty, Rogers' son, complying with his father's wishes closed up shop and sold the various items in the museum at auction.

The most popular of these items was Trigger who had been mounted at the door to the museum. The horse had had a career all of his own which began with his being ridden by Olivia de Havilland in the movie "The Adventures of Robin Hood". After this stirring beginning, Rogers purchased the horse for $2500. and the pair made almost two-hundred movies together. The horse's saddle and bridle sold for the sum of $386,500.

Also located within the museum was Dale Evans' horse Buttermilk, a Quarter horse with milky-white buckskin coloring. He was ridden by Evans in the television series of the 1950's "The Roy Rogers Show" along with Trigger. Both horses were so popular that statues, pictures, lamps and many other items were bought by children and adults.

Roy Rogers had gone to Vietnam years earlier to entertain the troops stationed there. His flight jacket was purchased for the sum of $7500. while letters and other personal items sold for $938.

Clothing and boots, of which Rogers had many, were purchased for over $20,000. Shirts worn by the star fetched more than $16,000. each while hats sold for over $17,000. Rogers car, a Bonneville, was auctioned off at over a quarter of a million dollars. Items purchased by fans of Rogers and his wife Dale Evans demonstrated the popularity of the stars well into the twenty-first century.

It has been said that the death of the Roy Rogers Museum was the end of an era that also included Gene Autry, Hopalong Cassidy, Captain Kangaroo, and "all those people whose lives touched ours, and made them better." So long and Happy Trails on the "great ride through childhood." It was a fantastic time to live, love and be alive.

Birds, Planes and Other Flying Things

Birds have fascinated men for centuries because of their ability to fly and soar through the air. Wilbur and Orville Wright from Dayton, Ohio were prime examples of this consuming interest resulting in their invention of the first airplane. This fascination led another man to study birds and draw exquisite pictures of them. The man was James Audubon and his pictures of these delicate creatures still draws audiences regardless of the fact that they are over a century old.

James Audubon was born in Haiti; his father supported the American cause during the Revolution. His son considered a naval career but suffered seasickness besides not liking the study of navigation while attending military school. Abandoning school, he pursued a study of birds for which he had had an affinity since a child. The boy would spend hours walking in the woods studying nature.

After the war Audubon's father and his family returned to France, but in 1803 immigrated to the United States. He settled first near Valley Forge but later moved to Kentucky. His son became a noted ornithologist writing about birds and painting their pictures supported by detailed notes. James Audubon subsequently moved to New Orleans but in 1826 sailed for England with over 300 drawings of birds each in its natural habitat. He was received enthusiastically by the British who called him the "American woodsman". This led to the publication of his famous book *The Birds of America,* a monumental work for which he is known. Costs of publication were over $100,000. King George IV was a strong supporter. Audubon wrote a second book about the ornithology in Labrador before returning to the United States where he was received with honor. His book became a best-seller and caused a park to be named after him in New Jersey.

Audubon worked in watercolor with chalk for bird feathers; the birds were placed in their natural environment on branches with berries or flowers.

Honor followed the man with the creation of the National Audubon Society in 1905 and a stamp in 1940 made by the United States Post Office. At a Sotheby's auction in 2010 a copy of his famous book sold for $11.5 million dollars.

People's fascination with birds and flying are apparent in the story of the Wright Brothers and their first airplane, also in the excitement of the air shows which have continued in the United States to the current time. Birds played a part in these shows since excessive bird activity in the Ohio area actually caused many of the shows to be cancelled on numerous occasions!

Air shows, also called air tattoos or air fairs have become a very popular form of entertainment in the United States since passenger plane travel became a standard mode of transportation early in the 1900's. Today's shows are held with several purposes in mind; often air acrobatics are a big feature of the show with pilots demonstrating flying skills in their planes. Some shows are put on by the military in support of events or charities while others are sponsored by businessmen seeking to advertise their wares.

The first air show was held in Rheims, France in 1909. Understandably the shows revolve around good flying weather; bad weather limits pilots with the stunts they can do. Air show season runs for a full six months in the United States when the weather is satisfactory for such an event to be held.

The air show evolved from long distance air races which were popular prior to World War II. Today's shows feature flying displays by jets used by the Blue Angels among other groups. Pilots demonstrate their skills in climbing to the heights, air plane rolls or speedy, dexterous turns. Safety is of primary importance both for the pilot and for the crowds gathered below although accidents do happen.

Toledo, Cleveland and Dayton are all involved in air shows which are popular with flyers in these areas. The Dayton show was a direct result of the Wright Brothers inventing their first airplane in Dayton, Ohio. Each year since the show began (early 1970's) thousands of people who love flying flock to this event which grew out of a General Aviation Day and later a Dayton Air Fair, all celebrating the history of flight in the Miami Valley. Pilots from the region who performed at the show included Harold Johnson and Bob Wagner whose wife Pat was a noted "wing walker", another stunt popular at these events.

The Toledo Air Show in 2016 was extremely popular and was attended by over 50,000 people who flocked to the Toledo Express Airport. The money raised was over $500,000. and went to charity; this enthusiasm on the part of the spectators almost guaranteed that the show will be returning in future years.

The Cleveland Air Show, generally held over the Labor Day Weekend, has enjoyed a fifty-year history of unique and unusual events from planes getting stuck in the mud, bad weather, and a marriage taking place. The first show was held in 1964 at Burke Lakefront Airport; these early shows were tied in with air racing. Another landmark was reached in 1970 when the event was opened to women competitors. The same year one of the pilots flew his plane down one of Cleveland's main streets, dodging the skyscrapers!

Unfortunately bad weather cancelled the show in 1975. Two years later future space astronaut John Glenn was the Grand Marshall of the event followed by golfer Arnold Palmer the following year. The Blue Angels and Thunderbirds performed feats in flying; in 1987 wingwalkers on biplanes were featured.

The year 1978 was an unfortunate year since a pilot, Bill Falck, died after his plane smashed into Lake Erie. Arnold Palmer was the Grand Marshall during the event. The following year was much happier with a skydiving clown named

Thunderchicken displaying his talents. A wedding also occurred during the show. In 1980 the British Air Force performed and a plane called Gossamer Albatross (named for the Coleridge poem) was on display for fans to view. A B-52 bomber and the Thunderbirds also performed. The following year the Goodyear Blimp stole the show while in 1985 the supersonic airliner the Concorde was the main attraction.

The year 1987 was the year of the wingwalkers, namely Johnny Kazian and Lori Ross who passed a baton back and forth on two separate bi-planes. Three years later a unique event occurred when the U.S. Navy Blue Angels shared billing with Otto, the talking helicopter! The Air Force Halcones from Chile made their one and only appearance at this show. Operation Desert Storm was featured in the airshow of 1991 with a fly-by by a Stealth Fighter and a display of the Patriot Missile System.

A noteworthy honor was bestowed on the Cleveland Air Show the following year when it was named "Air Show of the Year" by "World Airshow News". President George Bush did a fly-by in Air Force One to open the event. Ohio weather had a disastrous effect in 1993 when the torrential rains common in the state caused a U.S. Army plane to get stuck in the mud! A celebration was held in 1994 since the air show had remained at Burke Lakefront Airport for thirty years.

In 1995 several unique events occurred besides a fly-by by a Stealth Bomber. Grand Marshals of the show were the five members of the Space Shuttle team, four of whom hailed from the state of Ohio. The four years later was characterized as the year of excessive bird activity. Fortunately all of the aircraft involved including the noted Blue Angels landed safely. The following year the show was ruined by unpredictable weather of fog and rain involving a Bomber Parade featuring the Air Force Thunderbirds and the RAF's Nimrod. Beautiful weather characterized the following year (2001) when Cleveland hosted the Blue Angels and a hang-gliding act.

There was a forty year celebration of the show at Burke Lakefront Airport in 2004. The following year was unique since the show became a team effort assisting the American Red Cross to help Hurricane Katrina victims. Fans celebrated the following year when a souvenir program complete with trading cards and a poster of the Thunderbird aircraft were introduced. A rocket car from the world-famous Euclid Beach Park was also displayed.

Unique events occurred over the next five years when fans got to meet the astronauts from Ohio in 2008 and enjoyed Franklin's Flying Circus the next year. A jet-powered schoolbus and a movie theatre housed in a trailer with thirty seats marked the 2011 show while 2012 celebrated the bicentennial of the War of 1812 between the United States and England. 2016 was nicknamed the Year of the Bat, specifically the Batcopter and the Batmobile from the hit TV series while the U.S. Air Force Thunderbirds stole the show again with their brilliant flying.

The question remains as to what is ahead for the future of the air show? As long as people remain fascinated with birds and flying and want to learn more about it, the air show will survive and prosper. It could be a very long time indeed judging by the popularity of this event which has successfully survived for over fifty years.

For the Love of a Cat

The rivulets of water streamed down the metallic roof and sides of the taxidermy shop, the many droplets sounding like miniature bullets from machine gun fire in their staccato-like regularity. Later, the misty cobweb gray sky would change to black as the weather worsened and snow, along with the early darkness of Alaska, made a nightmare-like maelstrom outside. Susan Wall knew the signs; she had lived in Juneau for most of her life and knew the symptoms of bad weather like she knew her own name. By tomorrow, there would be inches of snow, regardless of the fact that it was only October. October in Southeastern Alaska, Susan reflected gloomily, meant precipitation; whether rain or snow was minute as far as she was concerned.

Susan watched her husband, Herbert, working over his taxidermy dissecting table. He mounted a wolverine, splitting it open rather like he would filet a fish and then finished it off by scraping all of the skin away from the inner flesh. Several small specks of blood oozed in a slow rivulet down the table, while the wolverine's now sightless, empty, eye sockets would be replaced with artificial glass, manufactured by a company in England.

Herbert continued his scraping of the flesh off of the skin, using precise, methodical strokes designed to get the job done with as little energy as possible.

"Herb, will you quit working for two seconds and listen to me?" Susan's greenish eyes beseeched the man who worked so diligently. "I didn't come up here to this forsaken place ten miles outside of town in this weather to watch you skin animals!"

Herb took his glasses off and dumped them next to the can of lukewarm soup which was his lunch. "What did you come for, Sue? I already told you I don't want any divorce. And I'm certainly not going to sign those..." he indicated the papers in her hand, "without consulting an attorney. Surely you and that Eddie fellow who works with you in the hospital pharmacy couldn't think I was such a country bumpkin as to do that!"

He glanced at Susan, his bald head gleaming in the glaring, overhead light like a shiny flat pancake. Susan knew he needed the light to stitch up the animal skins for his customers, but the dazzling brilliance did nothing to conceal the warts on his hands or the scar running along one side of his jaw. She'd asked him about the scar one time;

he'd said that a scalpel had slipped when he had been sucking the bones out of a small-sized squirrel. The knife had hit bone and scored a seam in his face. Score one for the animals, Sue thought now. Too bad he hadn't taken it as a bad omen and gone into another line of work.

Why had she married him? Susan wasn't sure. Looking back on it, she thought the answer was likely pity. She'd felt sorry for him, lying in anguish in the hospital where she worked as a nurse, with a ruptured appendix and nobody to give a hang to even bother sending flowers, cards or visiting. And for reasons that Susan barely remembered, he had touched a chord inside of her. Perhaps it was part of the Florence Nightingale syndrome that made her such a good nurse. At any rate, she had married him two months after his discharge from the hospital.

Herb pushed the wolverine aside and finally looked her full in the face.

"Have you found someone else, Sue? Is that what's behind this sudden yen for a divorce?"

"Herb, it's not a sudden yen. I made a mistake. I just can't take being stuck out here in the middle of nowhere. It would be different if we'd lived in town." Susan paused. Her eyes traveled to the shelves surrounding the counter with the cash register, where she used to wait on customers. The glassy-eyed animals stared back from those shelves, cold, lifeless, so…dead. Sometimes when she had come downstairs at night, it seemed as though the eyes followed her from one end of the store to the other. And the smell! It haunted her dreams; the smell of death and of the pickling crystals used in preserving the skins. One night she had found a squirrel soaking in salt-water in the sink. Her scream of anguish had brought Herb on the run. He had never cleaned any of the animals there again, but the damage had been done; Susan had used water from the shower to wash from then on.

Herb stared at her now, his dark-blue work shirt and pants covered with a red-splattered white apron. It was the same sort of apron they used in the morgue at the hospital, only for dead people, not dead animals.

He had started to speak. Susan Wall tried to focus on what her husband said.

"You can't say I haven't provided a good living for you. Isolated though we may be. Hunters, fishermen, even the big wheels from Seattle who come up have their game mounted here. Do you have any idea what I grossed last year? Triple what you make at the crummy little nursing job of yours! And I'm going to do even better this year!"

"That crummy little nursing job." Suddenly Susan wanted to scream out at him that at least she spent her time among the living at her job, not skinning and stuffing dead animals all day.

Susan wearily closed her eyes, trying to block out the dead wolverine and all of the others from her gaze. Herb took her silence as agreement with him.

"You could come back, Sue. I still care about you. And we got along so well." Herb stopped in mid-sentence. It was true, he defended himself mentally. They had gotten along just fine right after their marriage and his recovery from the appendicitis. The only sour note was Susan's little cat, Sparky. Sparky and Herb had been like oil and water, really, until Herb had removed the problem once and for all. Sue had never suspected and Herb, in a show of forgiveness for the nasty little kitty's bites and nips, had mounted him as a surprise gift to his wife. He'd though it most caring. After all, hadn't Roy Rogers had Trigger stuffed? Unfortunately, Susan had felt very differently about the whole thing.

She looked at him now. "Did we Herb? I thought I loved you," she said slowly "but after Sparky..."

"Sparky?" Herbert dropped his eyes, while his hands nervously played with one of his knives. He should be putting the wolverine skin to soak and be starting on the salmon, but quite suddenly, he felt frozen in place at the dissecting table. Did his wife know, he wondered? Did she know that he had helped the little cat along the road to kitty heaven? He raised his hooded, sphinx-like blue eyes to meet her green ones. No, it wasn't possible! He had been so careful. And yet...

Susan leaned sideways in the birch-bark chair that cut savagely into the base of her spine. "I was wondering, Herb. If you were still having those bad dreams like when we were first married. You did a lot of talking, Herb. About a lot of things. Interesting what I learned concerning your waking moments. They seem to have been almost as unpleasant as your time asleep."

Herb picked up the soup can and began spooning the rich tomato soup into his mouth. A trickle of it ran down his chin. Susan watched him quietly. Old habits never died, she thought to herself. Finally the can was empty. He pitched it half-way across the room to lie with the other trash surrounding the trash-bin.

Herb turned back to Susan. "No divorce, Sue. I mean it. And...maybe we could get another cat, if you like. One is pretty much like another. Only a bigger one, perhaps. He might like me a bit better and be a good guard cat, too."

To guard what? She looked at Herbert's billiard-ball head and almost gagged. Whoever said bald was beautiful had never seen her husband. Maybe on Yul Brynner or Telly Savalas, but on Herb? Never! And as for poor little Sparky...Herb had given her the answer in his dreams as to how her Sparky had really died. And he looked guilty!

Lucky Herb didn't play poker; he didn't have the face for it. But Susan knew she did.

Now she carefully rearranged her features. "All right, Herb. You win. No divorce." She jammed the papers into her overlarge tote bag and extracted a bottle of Australian wine. "Maybe you're right," she murmured slowly. "We should give it another chance. Let's drink on it to celebrate."

"Now you're talking!"

Susan forced herself not to pull away as he stroked her fingers.

"We need some glasses, Herb."

"Right." He moved back into the tiny nook that served as a kitchen. Susan could hear the water running as he quickly rinsed out a couple of dirty glasses. She tried not to think about what might be soaking in the sink.

Susan popped the cork on the bottle and poured a healthy amount into Herb's glass. Herb downed it like it was water while she sipped delicately at her wine. He finished off the bottle, smacking his lips over her choice.

"Those Aussies know how to grow grapes."

"I'm glad you enjoyed it, Herb." Susan watched her husband under hooded lids.

"And you did mean what you said? No divorce? You agree?"

Susan's hand crept into the pocket of her suede jacket and fingered the empty bottle of seconal, along with her husband's glasses, which were missing from the table. It had been so simple to slip the drug into the red soup and the wine...well...alcohol would just finish things up nicely.

"Oh, no, Herb." And Susan smiled as she rose to leave. "We'll never be divorced. I promise."

The wind whipped past the door as she opened it and let herself out, while a sinful smile played across her pale lips. The rain had half-changed to snow and the temperature had dropped. Susan squished over to her jeep; the light faded due to the coming Alaskan winter. It would be dark soon, regardless of the fact that it was only four o'clock in the afternoon. Susan clambered into her car and accelerated rapidly to the highway leading back to Juneau. She would have to thank Eddie in the pharmacy; he had turned out to be a good friend and true animal lover, like herself.

Herb listened as the car pulled away. Perhaps he should have invited Sue to stay over. But no, it was too soon. Once she had truly understood that he would not consider a divorce...

He moved to get back to the dissecting table, but suddenly something seemed wrong! His vision swam and his hands and legs felt wobbly and uncoordinated. Herb felt around on the table; where were his glasses? He was half-blind without them! His nearsighted cow-eyes searched around the table; then he crawled around on the floor. No glasses! Where could they be? They had been right here on the table when Susan first sat down.

Herb rose unsteadily, shaking his head slowly. His vision blurred, then cleared, then blurred again, while his head felt like someone with a sledge-hammer pounded on his skull Aspirin, that's what he needed! He'd drunk the wine too fast. A few aspirin would be just the thing!

Herbert half-dragged, half-walked back to the kitchen and swallowed half-a-dozen pills. His foot sliced at the empty can of soup, shoving it farther across the room. As he bent to pick it up, the room spun around like the wind in an Alaska vortex roaring off the mountains; he fell back and hit the floor before finally pulling himself erect and staggering back to the main room.

The walls of the cabin were moving inward; the tin sides seemed to undulate back and forth, like a snake he had once mounted, gorging on its prey. He searched again for his glasses, but they had vanished and now the room swung around like a top. Herb gagged, but was unable to help himself by vomiting. The spinning just got worse, along with the pounding in his head. Then his red-rimmed eyes focused on the mounted heads on the walls.

They were all there, sitting in a neat row like little soldiers on parade. He toasted them with the now empty wine glass. Granted, he could barely see them minus his glasses, but he knew where each and every one was. The buck's head in the far corner right next to the fish, with another squirrel in front. And the birds; the eagle that was from the museum over in Anchorage, a noble, majestic bird, as the founding fathers had said, with its glass eyes and outstretched wings, waiting to capture its prey.

The bird moved. Not a lot, but the wings half-shuddered, as though the eagle was infused with life once more. Herb blinked his eyes and rubbed a hand across his forehead. His face dripped with sweat; his shirt was drenched as though he'd been out in the rain. It was a draft, he thought, just a draft. His eyes blurred again as the bird flapped its wings and turned its head in his direction; glass eyes pinning him to the floor as if he had suddenly become the prey.

"No, you're dead! Dead!" Herb started backing away, slowly, one step at a time. He plowed into his dissecting table and felt one of the skinning knives turn into his back. His eyes blurred once more with tears as he scrubbed at them vigorously. His legs trembled uncontrollably, shaking, like a fawn first learning to walk.

The bird flapped its wings once more, almost in preparation for flight.

Herb's mouth gaped open but no sound was forthcoming. His mouth made strange guttural noises like primate man before learning to speak. His arm struck the table a glancing blow; skinning knives and the foam plastic used for the interior of

186

the mounts after they were skinned scattered haphazardly around the room. But Herb barely noticed them; his attention remained focused on the eagle as it turned its head slowly, from side-to-side. A proud bird, lord of all it surveyed. Then the eyes zeroed in on him, caught like an ant on an open anthill. Herb swore he saw life in the piercing eyes, as the bird once more lifted its wings in preparation for flight.

"No!" Herb began staggering slowly, like a drunken man toward the door of the shop. He stumbled and fell on the empty wine bottle that

had somehow gotten left and rolled off the table. The glass ground painfully through the heavy jeans that he wore and into his skin, but Herb barely felt the pain. He was totally engrossed in the mounted bird as it ruffled its feathers and lifted off of its perch, the lifelike wings carrying it straight toward Herb.

The man staggered erect once more, reached the door and yanked it open. Cold air flooded into his face along with a burst of snow as he slammed the door behind him. There was a crunch as though something solid had smacked into the metallic door. This merely increased Herb's fear as he slid uncontrollably toward the lean-to where his Hummer was parked. Yanking on the locked door, he groaned aloud. The keys were back inside on a hook by the back door. Herb looked at the exit through which he had just come. There was nothing between heaven or hell that would make him return inside.

He dragged himself slowly down toward the main road, which was quite apiece away. Sue had been right about one thing; the place was too isolated. She had described him once as a mole living in a moldy, above-ground hole. Herb had vehemently disagreed. He looked again at the distant road. Perhaps he could get a ride into Juneau. Perhaps...

He skittered along the muddy path, as the half-rain, half-snow increased, striking his face with sharp little needles. The cold bore into his bones as he staggered, like a grotesque drunk, toward the highway.

His strength was giving out as he chanced a last look back at the taxidermy shop. He squinted against the blinding tears that were flooding his eyes. Herb swore he saw movement behind the plaid curtains, which Sue had hung and which were a mockery of their married life together. A long beak with those piercing, eagle eyes followed his half-blinded course.

He chanced another look, unable to draw his eyes away, and never saw it coming. He slid on the wet, glassy rock, slippery from first the rain and now the snow. He scrambled frantically sideways, fighting for a hold which wasn't there.

The chill wind whipped violently, scattering puffs of snow. Herb thought back to his childhood reading; Jack London's "To Build a Fire" came to mind. He felt in his apron for matches and then groaned. They were back on the workbench in the shop, along with an ax for cutting wood. And with the wet...

Then he was falling, falling and rolling down the hill. Something crunched as his body hit more solid rock. His last conscious thought was that Jack London's hero hadn't make it out alive either. Then his head slammed backward and Herb knew nothing more.

Two weeks later Eddie March carried a small cat home from the hospital in a basket his friends from the pharmacy had drummed up. Someone had dropped the poor little kitty off in the snow-covered parking lot behind the main building and kept right on going. Eddie, being a kind-hearted sort of guy, had been elected to take the little animal home.

The weather had taken a turn for the worse, Eddie thought, as he drove carefully up Glacier Highway to his house overlooking the channel. There was a light on in the window welcoming him and the little stray home. Susan opened the door when he was halfway up the walk.

Her eyes lighted up with pleasure when she saw the cat, as Eddie shed his heavy overcoat and gloves and dropped them onto the nearest chair.

Susan fondled the kitten while Eddie went to fetch some fish from the refrigerator.

"We could call her Patsy Ann," Eddie spoke out. Patsy Ann had been immortalized in bronze in Juneau's Marine Park, as an abandoned animal who met ships for the rest of her life, looking for her absent owner. "Or something else, if you'd rather."

Susan scratched behind the cat's ears and was rewarded with a soulful look from the dark eyes. She hugged the little animal closer.

"No. I'd like to call her Sparky. After...you know..."

"Sure, honey." Eddie plunked himself in a chair, his white lab coat scrunched around his legs. "I just wasn't sure you'd want to be reminded."

"The times with Sparky were some of the happiest in my life. It was all the rest that turned into a nightmare, especially after I discovered that Herb had poisoned her." Susan paused. "The police came around again. Herb finally turned up, frozen, under a pile of snow. Some guy who wanted his wolverine mounted called the police when he couldn't get Herb for over two weeks. The cabin was a mess. The police don't know what to make of it, and after being frozen in the snow for two weeks, Herb wasn't much help. They can't figure why he ever left the shop and the car in such vile weather. They are calling it 'death by misadventure.'" The two accomplices stared into each other's eyes.

"Are you sorry?"Eddie asked softly, watching Susan with the cat.

"No, I'm glad. After all, Herb did say there would never be a divorce." She smiled at Eddie over the top of Sparky's head. "Well, he was right. There never was." And Susan pulled the newly christened Sparky toward her and began feeding the cat sardines off of her fingers.

Cardinals of the Brandywine Valley

She was a sleek, gray kitty with a long tail and golden eyes. She was also a stray who came to eat nightly as though she were starving. I'd named her Gray Lady for her beauty and friendliness and wondered how someone could callously throw her out on the streets. I couldn't understand how someone could have just thrown any of them out, the seven or eight cats that daily haunted my feeder, gobbling down the cat chow which my own three kitties had not eaten.

The cardinals watched over them, the famous cardinals of the Brandywine Valley off of Brandywine Road in north central Ohio. Their light red wings flitted across the trees almost like red leaves in the wind.

There were many legends about these beautiful birds. The most popular said they were angels in disguise and where cardinals lived, angels were sure to follow. Also called the Red Bird and the Virginia Nightingale, they remained in the valley all winter, never going south, feeding on the seeds, corn and grasses in the region. Their songs were sweet and lovely to hear. The males with their red feathers and the smaller, grayish brown females would build nests of dried grasses close to the many lakes and rivers where they would be frequently seen getting water. The birds mated in the spring with the smaller female sitting on the four to six eggs in the nest while the male jealously guarded them. The State Bird of Ohio was notoriously sweet-natured and never shunned contact with people in the valley.

I'd just put food into my cat dishes with Gray Lady, Bitty Tiger, Snowball and the other kitties milling around. One of the cardinals swooped down almost at the feet of Gray Lady. As I shouted a warning, she shot out a paw and broke the neck of this beautiful bird. I stared in horror as she grasped her prize and headed toward the local drainage ditch. I followed in hot pursuit. It made no sense to me; animals did not kill without a reason. Gray Lady had food and yet...

She reached the ditch with its old pipe and threw the bird down almost like a sacrifice. Then I saw them, the three gray kittens, images of their mother as they tumbled from their pipe and devoured the bird. Mother Cat stood guard which I understood since she was protecting the kittens against other animals, who were not friendly.

"You can bring them to my feeder to eat." I told her quietly. Yet they were so small, so defenseless against the coyotes, eagles and other predators that inhabited the Valley. Their mother had hunted food for her children as all mothers would do so they wouldn't starve to death.

I put cat chow down by their ditch for several weeks until the day the kittens followed Gray Lady to my feeder. They gobbled the food down, Little Grayling, Gray Boy and Graylee. I watched them grow stronger over the next weeks.

The cardinals from the Valley flew overhead and perched in my magnolia tree, watching the little ones as they became as beautiful as their mother.

Staying low, perhaps they knew, the sacrifice one of the birds had made to preserve these lives. I wouldn't have been surprised; they were very special birds with angel wings and more perhaps, who could be sure? As to the red cardinal who had sacrificed his life, I knew in my heart the very special person that he really was, the same person who had sacrificed himself for all mankind.

Linda Lehmann Masek

SPECIAL SECTION:

PHOTOGRAPHS

Hi, I'm the author, Linda Masek. When arranging the stories in the book, it seemed best to use only illustrations, as I had created special ones for each story. That worked well, but it seemed a shame not to share with you all the photographs I had taken (plus a few from other sources) Thus, this added section. I hope you will enjoy them.

Ducks swimming on the lake at Pickle Bill's Restaurant

197

My beloved Tweaky at her private window.

Linda with Maggie.

The Little Strays eating from one of the bowls of food provided by the author.

The beautiful black Siamese "Talker"

The author petting a baby seal in the far north.

More baby seals.

The peat fields on the Falkland Islands

A totem pole on the Falkland Islands

The town of Port Stanley in the Falkland Islands

Blue Goose Hotel in Port Stanley

A propeller airplane at the Fremont Airport

The tower at the Cleveland Airport

Roy Rogers and a fellow actor with horse Trigger.

Walt Disney United States postage stamp.

Balto, the statue of a Hero

Statue of the Blessed Virgin

The Shrine Honoring the Blessed Virgin.
A Statue of St. Francis stands beside the Shrine

St. Francis with the Animals

Kitty Tails II

Linda Lehmann Masek

Linda Lehmann Masek with Bunny

Born in Cleveland, Ohio, while studying to be a concert pianist with virtuoso Fred Kaiser, Linda took time out to become a certified scuba diver, a jet skier, a world traveler, a gardener, an English teacher, a published writer and, perhaps above all, a rescuer of animals.

Graduating from Nordonia High School, having been active in band, choir and the National Honor Society, Linda received two college scholarships for college. While in graduate school, she worked for the Western Electric Company in Solon, Ohio. She also began teaching handicapped students and realized that teaching was what she really wanted to do.

Linda received a full scholarship to Case-Western Reserve University for a postgraduate degree, a Master's in Library Science. After putting that degree to work for the next ten years in the Cleveland Public Library, she returned to school to pursue a second Master's Degree in History from Cleveland State University.

After graduation, a multitalented Linda, taught at private schools in Twinsburg and Solon, Ohio, before volunteering to teach at a private school in Northfield, where she remains today.

A prolific writer, Linda has published hundreds of magazine articles, along with fourteen books, all the while being a full time caregiver to her mother and taking care of her current three rescue kitties and a number of strays in her neighborhood. They are the inspiration for Magnificat!

Thanks

The author wishes to thank the following individuals and institutions for providing source material for many of the stories included in this book:

British Broadcasting Corporation (BBC);
Bernhart, Lucas, Combat Cat in USA Weekend,
    Cleveland Plain Dealer, Sept. 12, 2014;
Binch, Jack, Utahbirds.org;
Cleveland Plain Dealer, Feb. 13, 2017;
    Sept. 2, 2018;
Coffee Pot Farm, alpaca ranch in Ohio;
Daily Mail, Sept., 2008;
Daily Mail News, U.K., Dec., 2008;
DeMarco, Laura, Cleveland Plain Dealer;
Eaton, Cyrus;
Father DeCrane;
Google books.com;
Martin, Perry;
Miller, Donna, Cleveland Plain Dealer,
    May 11, 2010;
Mirrotto, Kitten Krazy Shelter;
News Leader, 2006;
New York Times, May 15, 2006; Jan. 29, 2019;

Noah's Ark Animal Sanctuary;
Purr-fect Place Gift Shop at Valley-Save-A-Pet
Animal Rescue Organization;
Wild Rose Rescue Ranch, Website,
Wikipedia;

Linda Lehmann Masek

68041971R00120

Made in the USA
Columbia, SC
07 August 2019